The Perfect Vessel

Haylee Brie

Published by Haylee Brie, 2022.

This is a work of fiction. Similarities to real people, places, or events are entirely coincidental.

THE PERFECT VESSEL

First edition. November 11, 2022.

Copyright © 2022 Haylee Brie.

ISBN: 979-8215391853

Written by Haylee Brie.

Table of Contents

This is dedicated to those who felt alone during rough times. Those who needed someone in their corner without a soul in sight. To those who allowed themselves to settle for less. For those in need of a little love

Chapter 1
The Monster Was Born

MY PARENTS WERE BORN in a land inside of the earth, called Ara. They believed that humans possessed a temporary vessel, a temporary version of themselves essentially. When you peel back each layer of the human, you would discover different parts of the universe. They were afraid of the universe because the universe was simply a large vessel for one large god. A god that was not a being of light. A god that believed in all thing's destruction.

Our people never traveled outside of Ara; we were never supposed to interact with the humans above. Humans believe that they are good and that demons live underground but they simply have never been told the whole story. We live longer than the average human life span. Our people always believed that we made more out of our 300+ years than humans in their 80-100 years. We were forced to go underground when Gods first creation gone wrong wreaked havoc on our land.

God became bored and started creating things that should have never been created. Dangerous creatures, these dangerous creatures took over our land. Our population diminishing making Moids minorities. It became a place of darkness; it became a hell. I've always been different, I'm not like the other Moids.

My parents named me Ara after our homeland because they always knew that I was special. My mother said that she could feel in her womb that there was something different about me. She said that she had a feeling that I would change Moid history, she just never knew how. She believed that I was destined to make change in some way, and that naming me after our land was the only name that she felt fit my essence. My parents weren't like other parents, they were different. My mom was a bit complex, but she is the only person that I've ever truly loved. Despite the things that she did prior to my birth, she's still very special.

I think she was failed somewhere in her life, which made her choose the path that she chose. But I always did everything in my power to make her proud.

My parents met when they were fairly young. My mom was two hundred and fifteen, and my dad was two hundred years old. They both always had a passion for others, who knows maybe it was really more of a fascination. They both loved seeing how people reacted to things, so they were always doing risky things. Since Moids have a long-life span, we have the ability to shed our skins and shift our appearance. You'd never know a Moids true age by their appearance.

THE PERFECT VESSEL

They bumped into each other in returning school and immediately felt a connection. Moids return to school many times throughout our lifespan, and both of my parents were very invested in their education. Mom was running late to her first class and abruptly walked right into dad, the both of them were in their own worlds. They were attracted to each other but neither of them tried to make any conversation at first. They ended up being late to the same class and sat directly across from each other. Mom has always been the bold type so when the class was over, she went over to him and told him that she wanted to know him. Dad smiled and told her that the feeling was mutual. They had lunch together and were together after that ever since. They were inseparable and did everything together. They couldn't keep their hands off of each other and were always doing things at inappropriate times. They were in love. The last time they were together in public mom didn't seem to be fully aware of what was going on around her. She says that she remembers that they were being really handsy in a classroom full of people, but they weren't the only ones doing it. She always emphasized that she clearly remembers that there were other people doing it too. Then the next thing she knows everyone that was in the classroom had disappeared, and she had no idea what happened to them. They were all dead, and dad told her that the both of them killed everyone. She had a hard time believing that she had anything to do with it because she had no recollection of anything that just occurred. Dad insisted that it was the both of them and made her help him clean up all of the evidence. She said that dad was moving with a sense of urgency because he knew that the police were on the way. She always felt like he was the one responsible, and that he wanted to pin it all on her. But by the time he made the call to the police, he couldn't bear the thought of throwing her under the bus. So, he told her that it was the both of them, and that they both enjoyed it. She says that while she was trying to hide and destroy all of the evidence, he seemed to keep zoning out. So, it forced her to have to do all of the clean up all by herself even though she had no recollection of committing the murders. She took all of the bloody towels that she used to clean and put them in school supply boxes in the teachers supply closet. As she was putting the last box up on the top shelf, the police came barging in and caught her attempting to hide the evidence. They were arrested on the spot and taken to a maximum-security prison. Prisons in Ara are different, they are all unisex. Since my parents were married at the time of the crimes, they were allowed to share a cell. But they were not allowed to be together at all times because it was still prison. They were happy even though their circumstances were rough, but they had each other. Mom always would say "all we needed was each other". Even though she believed that dad was responsible for the entire ordeal, she loved him no less. They were soulmates, she loved him no matter what. Their love is eternal and unconditional. After five years of being in captivity, they conceived me. I was born in prison but raised on the outside. One of the security guards had a close bond with my mom and offered to raise me and take care of me. My parents were still involved in my life, but I was able to be exposed to the outside world. I was blessed to have two moms and the coolest dad ever. I'll always love and cherish my parents, despite what they did. To this day no one really knows what happened that day except for my dad. He never planned to disclose the truth until his death. He wrote in great detail the specifics of what happened that day and included in his will that the letter will to be opened five days after his death. He didn't care about the public knowing the truth, that never mattered to him. He loved my mom so much, he just never wanted to disappoint her. He hated himself for never being able to provide her the life that he felt she deserved. He said that the moment he laid eyes on her he felt within his soul a shift within himself. He felt a twinkle in his heart. That twinkle in his heart gave him a vision of what his future would look like. Dad was quite his whole life, he never felt like he had much to say. He loved to observe and reflect on everything going on around him. People always described him as shy, up until the day that he met my mom. She brought out a side of him that his own parents never even knew existed. He became so full of life, like a spark had ignited inside of him. It was like he was reborn. He found his soulmate, he reconnected to his other half. Mom was the complete opposite of dad, but when they came together, they became everything that the other lacked. They became one. Dad enjoyed every day he spent with my mom, regardless of their circumstances. He never got to buy them their first house, or even raise their child the right way. He wanted to give her so much, but instead he took away her freedom. He hated himself for that, but mom was filled with all of what he lacked for himself.

I'll never forget the day that my dad died, that was the most horrific day of my life. Not only did I lose my dad, but I lost my mom too. Dad had a birth defect, and he was never supposed to make it far in life. His life expectancy was short, but he believed moms love extended it. He died suddenly, and five hours later my mom passed away too. They were one, and their death proved that. Five days after I lost my parents, I read the letter that he wrote for me. It broke my heart and changed me forever.

THE PERFECT VESSEL

Dear Ara,

If you are reading this that means I'm gone. I'm so sorry son. I hate that this was the life that I brought you into. This was never what I wanted for you. I was supposed to raise you. I missed your first steps, your first word, and even your first bicycle fall. I was never on the outside to do the fatherly things that I was supposed to, and that always ate me up inside. I wish that I could have given you and your mother the life that you'll deserved. I wish that I was different, I wish that I was better. Before I met your mom, I was different. I was the weird kid growing up, the odd one out. I never fit in anywhere, I wasn't normal. I had thoughts about hurting other people, and I didn't know how to control them. I felt like maybe I was part human, maybe I was evil. Maybe I came from somewhere else, but there was something wrong with my brain. I couldn't help the way that I was. I started to act on my impulses, but I never got caught. It became so easy to get away with what I was doing, that I became addicted. I want you to know the truth. It was me that killed all of those people, it was me son. Your mother had nothing to do with it. To be completely honest with you, I drugged your mother because I felt the impulses coming on. I didn't want her to witness what I had done. I'm telling you this because I'm afraid that I may have created a monster. I'm afraid that I have passed down this head sickness to you. I found someone that helped me control my impulses, so son you must get out there and find your person. Find your other half. I don't want you to end up like me. Enjoy your life, live it to the fullest, and do it soon. I know that your mother suspected the truth all along, but I couldn't bear the thought of her suspicions being validated. Don't put another woman through what your mom went through. She deserved better, but I'm just so glad that she had you. The best son in the world. I love you son, and I hope that we meet again.

Take care of yourself.

Dad.

Chapter 2
Cherokee

IT'S FUNNY HOW A LITTLE black line on my eyelid can change my entire face. Without that little black line, I look like I've never gotten any sleep in my entire life. Without that little black line, I look lifeless. That little black line gives me just enough confidence to get up and go about my day. Without it I'd feel so bare, like my true colors may start to bleed out. That little black line defines me. I don't know who id be without that little black line. Confidence can really make or break a person's vibe.

My vibe is okay, just okay. I stay to myself, but people tend to gravitate to me. And without my little black line, I'm afraid I'd be alone. I'm afraid that no one would find me appealing or approachable. I don't think I give off the most inviting vibe anyway, but maybe that's just the image I've created in my head. Being in my twenties is hard enough. Trying to navigate in a world where people arc defined by their careers.

Well screw that, I'm defined by me. My appearance and my personality define me, not what I do. People don't like the way that I live, and when I say people, I mean my family. I was always expected to be the golden child, but I could never live up to that label. I hate for people to have expectations of me because I refuse to live in a box. I refuse to let assumptions and other people's ideas dictate my life. Sure, I was a child prodigy, but that never defined me. It didn't matter how hard id fight it, my family continued to try to throw me into a box. "Cherokee will be this, Cherokee will be that". Why not just let go and see who Cherokee becomes without having people up her ass twenty-four seven? They never thought about how that made me feel; or maybe they did, they just didn't care. Having to live up to those type of expectations can really ruin a girl. What other fifteen-year-old math prodigy is addicted to cigarettes and coked out behind the bleachers? I was involved in every extracurricular activity that you can possibly think of growing up.

I was invited to all sorts of exclusive science camps and this and that. Apart of me feels like my parents put me in all that stuff just to get rid of me, but I know that they really did it for the image. Oh Cherokee got accepted into this program and that program OUR LITTLE GIRL. Our smart little girl. But your smart little girl needed guidance. Your smart little girl needed someone, and she never had anyone. So, your smart little girl turned to substances, the highs had my back. My parents were so disconnected from reality; they never even noticed that when I won the national spelling bee I was high off my ass, stumbling across the stage. Oh, it's just exhaustion, they'd say. No, I was broken and I needed you. But no one was ever there.

They finally noticed that I wasn't well, but by then it was too late. I had gotten ahold of some narcotics and took a few too many. I remember the look on my mom's face when I woke up in the hospital, I'll never forget that look. Instead of being genuinely concerned for my wellbeing, the look on her face was disappointment. It was now public how messy our family truly was. They could no longer cover up what was really going on, the truth was finally out. To be honest I was happy the truth was finally out. I wasn't this perfect little angel, and our family was far from perfect as well. I hoped that this incident would make my parents pay more attention to me, I wanted them to finally see me. But they never did, they never saw Cherokee. They only saw awards and metals. They looked at me and saw potential achievements, and each time they looked at me id break a little. I avoided my parents a lot as a child, but they always brushed it off as one of my quirks. I don't think people truly understand how our childhoods really shape us into who we become as a person. I give my parents very little credit to my positive qualities, because I feel as though I had to create them myself. My parents left me alone to fend for myself, and only showed up for appearances. I'll never forgive them for that, but I do miss them sometimes. They both died in a car accident when I was 22, which so happened to be the year that I sobered up. I had a feeling that big change was coming that year, but I'd never imaged that it would be losing the people who created me. Although we had our challenges, I still loved them. They were all I had for a while, even when I didn't really have them at all. They deprived me of so much, but maybe that is why I live the way that I do now. I live each day to the fullest, at least my own weird version of that. I don't live for the outside world or other people's approval. No one really cared about the stuff that really mattered, just the stupid surface level shit. I'm happy to have found myself, and I'm happy where I ended up. I know that I have my whole life ahead of me, so I don't need to have it all figured out. My parents always had this clear vision of what they wanted my future to be. But I never felt aligned with their vision. Deep down I've always wanted to be an assassin, but I don't think I really have the guts to end someone. But Idea of it kind of excites me. I don't know why everyone thinks that young adults should have to have their entire lives figured out in their twenties. Our brains are still developing, we are coming into ourselves. Why should we put all of this pressure on ourselves, that doesn't seem fair to me. Honestly when my parents passed away a part of me felt a great sense of relief. I was relieved that I no longer had to try to live up to their unrealistic expectations. I was relieved that I could finally really explore who I want to be as a person. I was relieved that I'd be able to fail a few times before succeeding without getting judged. Don't we all deserve that? I was relieved that maybe in their absence id somehow be given the opportunity to just live, and I have done just that. My parents left me a lot of money, and for that I am forever grateful. To be honest I have enough money to last an entire lifetime, and that helps ease the moments that I miss them. Because now thanks to them, I am not pressured to do anything. I live in my childhood home, that's been in my family for generations. I have literally no responsibilities, life is great. I am sober now but I'm happy about that. I am happy that I found me, I just hate that it took my parents dying for me to get to that point. But things are great, I think this has been the best year of my life. I met my best friend this year, and she's taught me so much. She's taught me about things that really matter. She's taught me how to live. I owe her everything, I don't know who I would have become if I hadn't met her. I go through these rough periods, but I get help for it now. Anna met me when I was in a place that I thought I wouldn't recover from, she keeps me above water. I don't do anything without her, I guess that's a part of my crippling abandonment issues. She talked me into going to see a therapist, she's truly godsent. Anna had a rough childhood too, but in different ways. Her parents beat her, well mostly her dad. He was an alcoholic, and he never wanted kids. Whenever he was drunk and laid eyes on her, he'd beat her senselessly because deep down he hated her. I think me and Anna are good for each other, I just wish that I met her sooner.

This year we decided to set goals, well she does it every year. But she's helped me come up with a few, she says it'll feel good just to be able to cross things off of a list. She's right, but sometimes I wish that I didn't set so many goals for myself.

I suppose apart of my parents will always live on inside of me. But today is my birthday, I don't want to think about my parents. I don't want to think about my childhood or sick and twisted parents. I deserve one day to be happy, one day to fully be at peace. I deserve one day to be celebrated.

I usually go for my signature cat eye liner look, all black, and gold jewelry. But it's my birthday, I want to shake things up. I'll wear blush and ill even try to contour a little. My jaw is oddly sharp, maybe I was supposed to be a boy or something. But ill contour just for the heck of it. Why not go all out? I'll wear mascara, but not too much. I never liked that caked on clumpy look, it's not my style. I'll even get a manicure, just because I deserve it. I deserve it to look pretty, I deserve to feel pretty. Maybe today will be my lucky day, maybe ill find a guy.

I've never had a boyfriend, but I've always wondered what it's like. I crave affection but have never really given the love scene much chance.

Guys have liked me here and there, but I never had much time to entertain. I graduated from high school really young and attended college before all of my peers. I guess that just comes with the territory of being a prodigy. My whole life has been dedicated to academics, all up until my parents died. After that day I decided to live for me. And ever since then, I've been at peace.

Chapter 3
And So It Begins...

ARA STARTED HIS MONDAY as he usually does, except something was different on this Monday. Ara felt a shift inside of himself that he couldn't explain, something was just different. Maybe it was his intuition alerting him that he needed to pay more attention to himself. Ara has been inhabiting his current body for five years, but this Monday he knew that he was ready for change. This feeling growing inside himself gave him a grave feeling of discomfort that he didn't know how to work through. He sat and stared at the ceiling trying to find answers with himself, but he came up with nothing. He needed to get out, he needed to clear his head. He needed a friend, his loneliness had started to drive him crazy. He knew he needed change, and on this Monday he was ready. He was ready to reinvent himself, to become whoever he needed to be. Because going another dreadful day alone would destroy him, at least that's how he felt. He wanted to do something different on this day. He wanted to look different, feel different, smell different. He had grown tired of himself, this was the Monday that changed everything. After he had his breakfast, he decided it was time to decorate. He stuck to himself, and he lived as if he was still in Ara. Never socializing or having company over. He never quite adapted to his new atmosphere, but it never bothered him.

This Monday was different, it was a day of reinvention. He knew that if he didn't want to be lonely, he had to make some changes. If he were to make a friend, he wouldn't want to invite them over to his depressing home. He needed to create an atmosphere that people would want to be in. He made a design plan of what he wanted his home to look like, it was beautiful. It was cozy and inviting, you'd never expect anyone other than a normal human being to live in such a beautiful place. But Ara was not human, in fact he was far from it. Ara made a list of everything that he needed to buy for his renovations and headed out to go shopping. He started with Home Depot, to get lumber and hardware. He went down the light fixture aisle because he had a vision in his mind of serene mood lighting. But he didn't find anything that really spoke to him.

While standing in the aisle trying to alter the vision in his mind, a man approached him. He asked him if he needed any help, Ara said no. But he did in fact need help. He wanted to share his vision with the store clerk to see if he had any recommendations, but his mouth stayed shut. As the clerk walks away Ara extends his forearm and knocks over the light fixtures in front of him. He starts to yell "see this is what happens when you can't get quality service! All I wanted was a nice lamp for my new apartment and no one could help me! Is that too much to ask for?" Ara proceeds to knock over multiple light fixtures in the aisle, causing a major scene. The clerk says, "sir I asked you if you needed help." No no no, that's not true. That's not true at all, you didn't help me. Why didn't you help me? I just want some lights, what do you want me to sit around in the dark or something? Aru says to the clerk. "Sir all you had to do was tell me what you wanted; from there I could have helped you. You are destroying all of this merchandise, you are going to have to pay for that. Pay? You want me to pay? Why do I have to pay? I am a customer seeking assistance, I didn't find what I needed. Why would I have to pay? You can pay! I'm not paying for anything, I don't want these lights. Ara says. "Sir either you pay for these lights that you've broken, or I'm going to have to call the cops. The choice is up to you." Come on man, we are just having a misunderstanding. Relax, it's okay. Ara says while placing his hand on the clerk's shoulder. "Sir, please get your hands off of me, this is very inappropriate. Either you pay or I call the cops, the choice is up to you." Ara runs away from the clerk and begins to throw things nearby as he's running towards the exit.

He made it out of the store untouched and made his way to his car. Ara often did odd things like this, he really did it for the attention. He loved the way it made him feel to have so many eyes on him. He didn't care how people perceived him, he just wanted to be seen.

He got in his car and drove to the mall, which was a forty-five-minute drive from home depot. Ara lived secluded in the mountains. Having no neighbors or nearby stores made him a bit lonely at times. He liked having his privacy though.

Ara listened to the same cassette tape every time he drove to town. He didn't like branching out to try new things. He replayed the same tape time and time again, and never grew bored with the repetitive tunes. He always dreamed of what it would be like to find love. He would daydream about it every time he drove, the tunes created fantasies in his head. He never felt worthy of love, he knew it was because he was different. Aru had a really off-putting energy about him, unless he was acting of course.

Aru was a very good actor, and when he met a human he was actually interested in, he'd pretend to be someone that he's not. He often introduces himself as many different names. Today Aru felt that he needed a physical makeover, just like his home. He knew the only way to make himself appear less creepy was to play the part of a normal human. Deep down he always wished that he was really normal, he wished that he was human. Ara pulled up to the mall and parked his car. He looked at his reflection in the car mirror and felt sad. He didn't want to be who he saw gazing back at him. He gets out and approaches Macys. He walks over to the beauty counter and asks the beautician for some advice. "Hi excuse me. I'm looking to change my look, a makeover if you will. I don't really know anything about fashion, style or girls. You see; I've never had a girlfriend, I've never talked to a girl in that kind of way before. Girls always sort of look past me, like they don't see me. I don't want to be invisible anymore, I want to be seen. I'm tired of being overlooked. I know that this is a makeup counter, and I am not looking for makeup. I really just wanted advice, from a woman's perspective you know?

THE PERFECT VESSEL

What could I do to make myself appear a little more appealing to girls?"

Well hello there. You seem like a sweet young fella, so I want to help you. I don't usually do this sort of thing, but I feel inclined to help you out. If you give me ten minutes, I can come help you . I've got one customer that I've got to finish up with and then I'll go on break. How does that sound? "Oh, that sounds perfect, thank you so much. I really appreciate you for this. I'm going to walk around for a bit, but I'll be back soon! I don't want to linger around the beauty counter and make women feel uncomfortable."

Ara gives the clerk a friendly smirk and strolls towards the exit of the store. He always wanted a lava lamp, but never felt adventurous enough to spice up his home until this day. He felt today was the perfect day to get one. Ara walks over to spencer's and asks the worker if they sell lava lamps. The worker says "We do, right over here I'll show you". Ara followers her closely, and the worker quickly turns around. "A little close there don't you think?" Ara smirks and says "I apologize. I didn't mean to get in your...personal space. Thank you for your help". The worker blushes and says to Ara "It's no problem, enjoy." And quickly scurries off. Ara knew that he had an attractive face. He just had to learn how to be charming ,and not have an off-putting energy. He usually doesn't care too much of what people think of him, but today was different. He felt that he needed to practice, he wanted to be able to make a friend. Most of all, he wanted to be able to find a girl.

Ara picks up the red lava lamp and takes it over to the cash register to pay. He pulls out his brown worn out wallet out of his back pocket, and drops all of his cash on the floor. The cashier runs around the counter to help him pick up all of the loose bills. Ara gives her a charming smirk and says "You're a good girl, aren't you? Thank you for helping me." The cashier blushes and says "Oh it's no problem. How come I've never seen you in here before? Are you new in town?" No; not new, I've been here for quite a long time. I just don't get out too much, I tend to stay to myself. I usually only go on outings if I need something. Ara says. "Well; you should come out more often, you're pretty cute you know. I wouldn't mind seeing a handsome face like yours again. Anyways I hope you come back soon, here's your change. Enjoy your lamp Mr...?" Tim, I'm Tim. I didn't catch your name. Ara says. "Bethany..Beth, its nice to meet you Tim." Aru gives Beth a flirtatious smile, "Timothy..Tim". I'll be seeing you miss Bethany Beth. The cashier chuckles and waves Ara goodbye. As Ara approaches the door to exit, he lays eyes on the prettiest girl he'd ever seen. He wasn't ready to approach her yet because he wanted to get some advice from the beauty clerk. He watched the beautiful girl walk past him while she talks with her friend. Beautiful long brown hair, and big brown eyes. He'd never seen such a beauty. Ara walked back over to the Macys to go see the beauty clerk. He didn't see her at first and started to turn around, and then he noticed that she took her hair out of her ponytail.

THE PERFECT VESSEL

She was almost unrecognizable, she was stunning. Ara walks over to her and as he approaches her, he combs his fingers through his ashy blonde hair. "Wow you let your hair down, you are truly stunning. I almost didn't recognize you. Not that you weren't beautiful, I just didn't notice you before." That doesn't fully sound like a compliment, but I'll take it. Thank you. I don't believe I caught your name. "Jonathon. Ara says. "Well Jonathon, it's nice to officially meet you. So, what exactly did you have in mind? "Well, you see, I've never been into fashion or anything. I've never had a girlfriend to help me out with my style, so I just wanted some help in that department. Girls hit on me a lot, but I don't always feel worth being complimented on because most of the time I know that I'm not dressed well." Well Jonathan, you are very handsome. I think that a simple blazer with a plain white shirt underneath would be a nice look for you.

I can show you a few if you have the time? Ara flirts. "Oh, miss I have all the time in the world for you." Oh stop it you're going to make me blush, follow me its right over here. Ara follows the beauty clerk as they walk over to the men's clothing section. "So, miss are you single?" I'm not, happily engaged. But I know you'll find the perfect girl for you. Let's get you dressed all nice and spiffy and I bet you'll find Mrs. Right soon enough. "Engaged? Oh man, what's that like? Can I see the ring? I sure hope that he treats you right." The clerk holds up her dainty hand to show the ring. It's not the biggest rock in the world, but I love it. I'm happy, and that's all that matters. You remember that for me, okay? You don't need some big fancy ring to propose to the girl you love! You get what you can get, and make sure you treat her right! Shell be the happiest girl in the world, I guarantee it! "I'm just glad you're happy, lucky guy". Ara says. The clerk approaches a mannequin that she thinks has the perfect style to fit Ara. "See this mannequin here, I can totally envision you in something like this. This looks like your style, do you want to try it on?" I'll take it, I trust your judgement. Would I be able to change into it after I purchase? Ara says confidently. "You sure may, let me ring it up for you Hun." The cashier rings up the outfit and Ara gets his wallet ready for payment. "You seem like a really nice man, I've got a special discount for you, okay?" Oh, thank you so much ma'am, I really appreciate your generosity. You have been so kind and so helpful. "You are more than welcome; I hope that this finds you well." I'll go change into it and come back to show you.

Ara changes into the new outfit and goes back to the beauty clerk. It fits perfectly , I actually really love it. Ara says. "Oh, you look so handsome, I'm so glad that I could help. If I had a single friend, I would totally hook you guys up. I hope you find your misses!" I know I will now with your help! Thank you so much. "It's not a problem, and just one piece of advice. I think your hair would look so pretty jet black, see if the salon has any color appointments available. I know you'll be stealing hearts soon! Don't be a stranger come and talk to me again soon, okay?" I will head over to the salon right now, thank you so much. I never caught your name.

Ara says. "Gloria, and don't forget it okay?" I'll never forget you Gloria. Ara smirks. Ara walks into the salon next door and gets his hair dyed. They only had one other customer, so they were able to fit him in for a same day appointment. After Ara leaves the salon, he walks over to the food court and buys an ice cream cone.

He strolls around the mall looking for the beautiful girl that he saw earlier while licking his cone. He begins to lose hope that he'll find her again and as soon as he finishes his cone he spots her. He walks up to her and introduces himself. "Excuse me beautiful ladies ,can I stop you for a minute? I saw you guys earlier and I wanted to come say hi, but you see I can be a little shy at times. I'm Jack, what are your names?" I'm Anna and this is my best friend Cherokee, she's a little shy too. Cherokee, what a beautiful name.

Chapter 4

New Routine

ARA WAS COMPLETELY in awe with Cherokee, he'd never seen such a beautiful human in his entire life. He knew that he wanted to have her, and would make that happen by any means necessary. He had to put his best foot forward, and try his best to leave a good impression. "Can you believe that this is my first time at the mall? Crazy how id run into such beauty on my first mall outing" Ara says. You've never been to the mall before? Have you been living, under a rock? Anna chuckles. "Something like that, I'm not from here. But enough about me, I'm very intrigued by your friend here Anna. What brings you guys to the mall today?" It's my birthday and I'm trying to pick out a nice birthday outfit, I don't really have any special plans though. "Birthday? Well happy birthday to you pretty girl! What do you say if I tag along with you guys? I can give you a guys perspective, or whatever. I don't really have many friends here, and you two just seem like really nice people." Oh well sure, I'm sure that could be helpful. So where are you from? And why have you never been to a mall before? They don't have malls where your from? "Oh they do, but they are very different. I've spent most of my adult life here you see, but I've always been shy. I've never mingled much, I've just stayed to myself. I always thought of a mall outing as something you do socially, you know like with friends. But I woke up today and decided that it was time for some change. I decided it was time to finally decorate my apartment, so I thought id go out of my comfort zone and come here." So you're a loner huh, me too. Cherokee says. Loner, I wouldn't say that. Well, I guess that would be the right terminology. Look lets check out this store, they look like they'd have some things that would look amazing on you. "I have the most perfect idea, you guys are going to love this. Why don't we have you come over and we can have a small little get together? We can dress up ;have drinks, play games, it'll be fun. What do you say?" Anna says enthusiastically. "I'm down if you are". Ara gazes deeply into Cherokees eyes. Cherokee looks at Anna and then responds to Ara. "Um yeah sure, I'm down. I just hope you aren't a creep or anything. Are you, you know a creep?" Cherokee says with concern. "Hey that's rude! Be nice, this is why you don't have friends! You don't know what's appropriate." Anna says. No its okay, I like a forward woman. A woman who isn't afraid to speak her mind regardless of how she may be perceived. I like that. Cherokee blushes. And to answer your question, no I'm not a creep. But if I was, I don't think I would tell you. Ara says. "Fair enough, you seem harmless. I still cant believe that this is your first time in a mall. Ill show you around to some cool spots after we find our outfits, sound good?" I'm down to do anything with you. Have I told you that you are just absolutely breathtaking? "Thank you Jack, you are kind. What do you think about this dress here? Its pretty right?" Cherokee points to a velvet red dress. "Yeah its alright, what about this one here? I think you'd look amazing in this, you should try this one on." Ara says as he points at a short black lace dress. "Its pretty, I like it. I don't think I could pull this off though, its too sexy. I don't think I'm sexy. "Cherokee says with uncertainty in her voice. "What do you mean you don't think you are sexy?! Have you seen yourself? I didn't want to come on too strong, but you are the most beautiful woman that I have ever laid my eyes on. And I really mean that, I do hope that I can get to know you. You are truly mesmerizing." Jack says reassuringly. "Oh Jack you are just saying that, don't try to flatter me. I think I will try it on though. Its my birthday and I should try the sexy look for once, at least for the day. "Cherokee says while removing the dress off of the hanger. "Sweet girl you are sexy on any day, go try it on you'll see." Cherokee blushes and takes the dress into the dressing room to try on. She removes each garment of clothing with a head full of doubt. She doesn't believe that she looks as good as her new friend is claiming. She has never seen herself as that pretty, at least not in the way he describes. She's never had someone be so forward and upfront so soon upon meeting. She really liked how he seemed fearless. He didn't seem to care what anyone thought of him, and he had no filter. It seemed like he said the first thing that came to his mind without taking a second to reconsider. She liked that about him, and from that it made her want to get to know him. She wanted to see if there was a connection, if there was any potential there. She put the dress on her frail body. She struggled with her body image on most days, and put herself on unusual diets. She looked in the mirror and felt more beautiful than she ever had in her entire life. She wondered if it was really the dress that made her feel so confident in herself, or was it the words of her new friend. Either way she felt gorgeous, and she became very excited of the night ahead. She opened the dressing room door to reveal to Anna and Ara the dress. Ara looked at her with googly eyes, but didn't say anything at first. His eyes widen, and he begins to slowly clap. "Now that is a woman. You are so unbelievably stunning. I just knew that you would look amazing in that dress."

"Yeah Cherokee, you have to get that dress, its gorgeous! You look so amazing!" Anna says. "Well happy birthday to me, ill go get my clothes so we can check out. I want to wear it out, do you think they'll let me? "Yeah they should be able to just scan the tag and just make sure they remove the sensor if it has one." There is one right under my boob. I've got to say Jack, you've got great taste. Thank you so much.

Cherokee walks over to the cash register to purchase her new birthday dress and Anna follows behind her. "Jack are you coming?" Anna says. "Yeah ill be right over, I was just looking at these shoes. They look like they would go well with the dress. What do you think? Ill get them for you, since its your birthday and all. What do you think Cherokee?" Oh Jack that is so sweet of you, I love them. Ara picks up the shoes and stands in line behind Anna and Cherokee. "So how far do you live from here?" Ara says. "Oh not far at all, I'm about fifteen minutes away. You can ride with Anna and I so you don't have to worry about driving if that's easier for you." What If it turns out that I am some kind of creep and you want me to leave? "Well that's not very comforting, but its okay I trust you." Cherokee says.

THE PERFECT VESSEL

Even though the two just met, Ara had already gained the trust of Cherokee. Gaining ones trust can sometimes be very difficult, but Cherokee trusted Ara immediately. She felt that they had a connection. She didn't want to say anything, but she felt like she had a crush on him already. They decide to take one car to go to Cherokees house to celebrate. They stop at the liquor store, and get three bottles of vodka. They were young and full of life, they wanted to really enjoy themselves. Cherokee felt like she may have found her future lover and she felt optimistic. She felt better than she'd felt in awhile. Ara offered to cover the liquor store tab, but the girls insisted that they just split it evenly. They felt that since they just met, it would be wrong to have him take on the whole tab. Especially after he just bought Cherokee her birthday shoes at the mall. Ara offered to buy them food as a nice gesture, and they mutually decided on tacos. There was a taco place right by Cherokees house so they stopped on the way in. Ara went into the restaurant by himself to place the order to go. "Hi I'd like to place an order to go, can I see a menu this is my first time here." Ara says. "Welcome, yes of course here you go." The waitress hands Ara a menu. Ara orders so much food, it looked as if he could be feeding a party of ten people. He wanted to impress Cherokee. He wanted her to have plenty of food and plenty of options. After he placed the large order of food, he walks over to the bench to sit to wait for it to be ready. A man from afar yells out "Hey I know you!" No I don't think so, I'm not from around here. You've got the wrong guy. Ara says. "No you are that crazy guy from Home Depot, I remember you. I would never forget you after that stunt you pulled earlier." You've got the wrong guy. Ara says nervously. "What are you having a party or something? Who would come to a party with a creep like you?" No like I said you've got the wrong guy. Anna walks into the restaurant to check on Ara to make sure everything is okay. "Are you with this guy here?" Yeah why? Anna says. "Be careful, this dude is a total whack job." The guy has mistaken me for someone else, don't listen to him. He says that he recognized me from home depot earlier today, but I never went to home depot today! I've spent the whole day at the mall. You've got to believe me, I'm not a creep or anything." Anna looks at the guy, and then looks at Ara. "I believe you, the guy seems a little off anyway. I just came in to make sure everything was okay, did you order the food already?" Yeah it should be ready in just a few more minutes. I kind of got a lot, I wanted to impress Cherokee. Ara says. That's cute, I appreciate you looking out for her. She really needs this you know. A nice day with a nice guy. She's been alone for so long, I'm all she has. I know we all just met, but I'm rooting for you guys. "Aw thanks, do you believe in fate. I just feel like maybe I was meant to run into you guys today. Its just a feeling you know, I feel a connection. I cant explain it really, just this energetic sort of thing." Yeah I know what you mean, I do believe. I believe that everything happens for a reason. I believe that we were at the right place at the right time. Just don't hurt her okay, she's really been through a lot. She deserves something good in her life, something wholesome. "If she gives me a chance, I wouldn't dare mess that up." Just between us, but I have a feeling that she will. Anna says.

The waitress tells Ara that the food is ready and waves him over to come and pay. "That'll be $165.45, how will you be paying today?" Geez what did you order? I can help with that if you want, that's a lot to spend on someone you just met. Anna says. "No its fine, she deserves it." Ara pulls his cash out of his wallet and hands the waitress exact change. "Ill cover the tip okay?" Anna says. "Sure if you insist, now lets go have the night of our lives" Ara grabs the food, the two walk out of the restaurant to the car. "Is everything okay? I was starting to get a little concerned, it took awhile." Cherokee says. No everything is fine, are you ready? "Sure lets get going." The three of them drive away, and soon reach Cherokees house. "Okay I'll grab the booze, Jack you can grab the food." Cherokee says. "Deal, is this your house? Its beautiful." Yeah it was passed down to me.

Ara and his new companions drink booze and eat tacos, they all become very comfortable with each other. Cherokee and Ara are laid out on the floor gazing into each others eyes, while Anna is passed out in another room. "You know I kind of have a crush on you." Cherokee says. "Really?" I mean I know that we just met and all but, sometimes a girl just knows." And what exactly do you know? " I know that I think you are really cute and I think you are cool. There is just something about you that is just very intriguing. I guess its your vibe or whatever, but there's just something about you that I like. And I know that you're funny and I know that you know how to have a good time. I like that in a person. So I know that I have a crush on you." Well Mrs. Cherokee I have a confession to make too. I have a crush on you too. I saw you in the mall and I thought you were the most beautiful girl in the world, that made me nervous. I didn't think I was good enough so I asked a woman in a department store for some advice. She picked out my outfit and cologne, and she even suggested that I dye my hair. I don't think I'd be this handsome if it weren't for her. But I wanted to look good for you, so that I could approach you.

Chapter 5
Captured

TWO MONTHS HAD PASSED since Ara and Cherokees drunken first night together. They told each other that night that they both had crushes on each other and wanted to pursue one another. They spent time together every day and hated being apart. They grew very close, they were inseparable. Ara knew that he found the one, and that gave him a great sense of satisfaction. He wanted to plan something special for her because it was their two month anniversary. He knew it wasn't really that big of a deal, it wasn't like it was two years. But he knew that this would be the night that he wanted to invite her to come live with him. Cherokee helped him decorate the kitchen and he allowed her to make many "feminine" sort of choices because he knew that one day she would be living there with him. The two of them had created a movie room, he intended to invite her over for movie night.

They had their first fight two weeks into seeing each other, which almost caused them to break up. But nothing could get in the way of the connection that they had. The day that they met he told her that he was at the mall shopping for décor for his apartment. This was partly a lie because Ara didn't live in an apartment. In fact he lived in an old mansion, which was quite nice. She didn't understand why he would say he lived in an apartment if that wasn't the truth. Small lies were a big deal for Cherokee, because she felt like if you can lie about something small than you can be lying about anything. She broke down crying because she felt like she had made a mistake by letting him into her life so quickly. She let him into her home when they had just met each other. She was afraid that she made a terrible mistake. The day after they got drunk on her birthday, Anna told her about the guy from the restaurant. Anna told her it was no big deal, and that the guy was probably crazy. But when Cherokee caught Ara in that lie ,it made her have this feeling In her gut. It made her feel like maybe that guy was telling the truth. Maybe he was some kind of wierdo. And she was so blinded with infatuation, that she completely overlooked the potential signs. Ara was able to calm her down and assure her that everything was okay. He expressed to her that he felt terrible about his lie, and that he'd never lie to her ever again. He kept his promise, but the fight stayed in the back of his mind constantly. He was so afraid that he almost lost her. He didn't know what he would have done if he lost her that day. Luckily he never had to find out, but it still bothered him. That's why he wanted to make this two month anniversary movie night 'special'.

THE PERFECT VESSEL

Ara set the mood in the entire house, not just the theatre room. He got fire wood for the fire place. He bought a new red light fixture to match the ruby red sofa better. He set up flowers around the whole house, he wanted to make it special. He wanted her to feel at home. After he was finished setting the mood in the house, he drove over to Cherokees house to pick her up. She wanted to drive but Ara insisted. When he arrived he fixed his hair in the car mirror, and quickly flossed his teeth. Then he stepped out of his car and walked up to her house to ring her doorbell. As he waited, he imagined what she might look like. Would she be wearing her birthday dress? She loved that dress, and he loved It too. Or would she be wearing something new that she picked out on her own. Shortly after his imagination went wild, the door opens and he lays eyes on Cherokee. Ara was starstruck by her beauty. She was wearing a beautiful ruby red dress, the same shade as his new light fixtures. It was silk, with a perfect V cut. Her bosoms popped out as if the dress didn't fit, but the dress did fit. It hugged her beautiful curves perfectly. She was wearing her birthday shoes paired with a dainty gold heart necklace. Her makeup done perfectly, not too much. She looked stunning, and this time she knew it. "You look so incredible". Ara says cheerfully. "Thank you, I thought you'd like this dress. Do you want any water or anything from inside, I know we've got a long drive ahead of us. "Cherokee asks. "No I'm good, all I want is you. Lets get going". Cherokee and Ara get in the car and drive back to Aras house.

When they arrive; Cherokee notices many trash bags outside of Aras house, which concerned her. She convinced herself that he was probably just doing some construction around the house, and that it was no big deal. Apart of her felt like there could be something bad in the bags, but she disregarded those feelings. She thought that if she even brought it up that it would cause them to get in a fight, and Cherokee didn't want them to fight on their special night. "What are you looking at? Are you ready to come in to see what I planned for us?" Ara says. "Oh nothing, I just spaced out for a second. I cant wait to see, lets head in." Ara and Cherokee walk inside to a candle lit house with vibrant flowers scattered around the floor.

Cherokees eyes lit up with such admiration, she knew she made the right decision that day at the mall. She wasn't the type to usually talk to strangers, but in this very moment she was so glad that she did something out of her comfort zone. "I have planned a movie night for us in the movie room of course. I've got all of your favorite movies lined up to be watched. We are going to watch them in the order that you told me about each one being your favorite. I remember every single time you told me about a different movie that you loved. I remember that gleam that filled your eyes as you told me about each and every one of them. "You remembered? You remembered all of my favorite movies? But how, how could you remember them all? You know I'm a crazy movie buff." Easy, because I love you Cherokee. "You...you do? You really do?" Yes Cherokee, I really do. I really love you. "Oh my gosh, Jack I love you too!" Aw baby kiss me. Ara and Cherokee share a passionate kiss, the best kiss of Cherokee's life.

"So, will you move in with me?" Ara asks while staring at Cherokee's wet lips. "What? Move in with you? It's a little soon, don't you think? I do love you, I really do. I just feel like it may be too soon, we can take this slow. There is no need to rush things right?" Oh, so you don't want to live with me. You don't really love me then? I thought you said you loved me? Ara says with disappointment. "No baby I do, it has nothing to do with our love at all. Its not that. I just don't know if I'm really ready. I mean I snore and, I don't really look that great in the mornings. I just want to take things slow, but I still love you. Okay?" Yeah sure, its no big deal. Today was still special nonetheless, we exchanged our first 'I love yous'. Speaking of special, I got you a gift. I got it for you incase you declined my offer, just so that you still have something special to remember this day by. Since I wont be giving you a key and all. Let me go grab it, stay put" Ara slowly walks into the next room over, and then looks over his shoulder at Cherokee. He picks up a gift bag and then walks back over. "So I really hope you like this, since you weren't too fond of my move in idea. I want you to know that I do love you." Lets see what you picked out, I know it'll be amazing because you have great taste. "Tell me that you love me first, I want to hear you say it. "Oh Jack, I love you okay. Now let me see what you got me! Ara hands Cherokee the bag.

Oh, this looks interesting. What is it ,some kind of high tech smart watch or something? "Here ill put it on for you, then you'll be able to see what it does." Ara gets close to Cherokee, and puts the watch on her left wrist. "Okay so what does it do?" Cherokee says with confusion. "Do you like it Cherokee? I made it just for you. It took me awhile, but I was determined." Um yeah of course, just show me what it does." Well here's the thing, its not a smart watch. Its not a watch at all in fact. "Jack why are you being like this, just show me what the watch does." I told you it is not a watch, and by the way my name is not Jack. "Okay now you are freaking me out, what is going on? I love you, please be honest with me." My name is Ara, not Jack. I am not human, I do not come from here. I am not from some little town that no one has ever heard of, because that doesn't make sense. That never occurred to you? Well either way, this is the truth. My name is Ara and I come from a land from inside of the earth. I have been here for awhile, but if I didn't find someone like you, then I would be forced to go back "You aren't making any sense, I don't know what has gotten into you. I don't know if your kidding or on some kind of drugs. But I do not find this funny, I kind of just want to go home now. Can we just do movie night another night? "You really are a silly silly girl. There is no movie night, and there is no going back home. This is your home now, so you are going to have to get used to it." Ara's demeaner completely shifts. "No I already told you that I am not ready to move in with you, remember? Or did you forget already?"

Ara slaps Cherokee with force. "Do I look stupid to you Cherokee? I did not forget what you said, I know what you said. I don't care what you said. We don't play by your rules, we play by mine. This is my world baby and you are just living in it. Got it?" Ara says. "You...you hit me. You really hit me Jack. How can you tell me that you love me, but you just hit me? I want to go home, this isn't funny Jack. "Little girl did you not hear me, I told you my name is not Jack. My name is Ara, and I come from a land from the inner earth like I said. I don't like to repeat myself. Please do not make me repeat myself again.

THE PERFECT VESSEL

Aras demeanor has completely changed, and is nothing like the 'Jack' persona that Cherokee fell for. She Is frightened and confused and has no idea what's going on. She doesn't want to get hit again so she doesn't ask. Instead she asks what the new watch is supposed to do, because he still hasn't told her. "Okay Ara, I'm sorry. I didn't mean to make you repeat yourself. This is just a lot to spring on a person you know, but I still love you. I just want to know what's going on that's all. What is this watch supposed to do?" I thought I told you, its not a watch. It is a device that I created with inner earth technology. My people are much more advanced than you humans. It is a device that will prevent you from leaving my property essentially . I thought that if I offered you to move in with me, then I wouldn't need to use it. But you see, I need to have you here. Whether you want to or not, that doesn't matter. What matters is me and you. And most of all, you. I don't want you to be afraid, and I don't want to have to hurt you. I did grow very fond of you, and I meant it when I said that you are the most beautiful human that I've ever laid eyes on. So now that we have a bond; and you've fallen in love with me I need for you to stay. "Why Ara, why do you need me to stay. I can come back everyday if you need to see me that bad, I don't mind. I want to see you often too." It is not about me wanting to see you, its not really about that at all. Its about me and my needs, and you fulfilling them for me. No one else can do it, because no one else is you. You are the one, you are the only one. And you will do as I say, and I don't want to have to tell you what will happen to you if you don't listen to me. But this is your home now, do you understand. "Can I use the bathroom, I need a minute to process everything. This is a lot, and I'm feeling a bit shaky. I'll be just a second." Rule number one, you will ask every time you want something or want to do something. If I say no then you must obey, no questions asked. If you question my decision, you will be punished. So to answer your question, no you may not use the bathroom. I do not believe that you really need to use the bathroom, I think that's a lie. Don't lie to me ,don't you ever lie to me Cherokee. Rule number two, if you lie to me you will be punished. Now Cherokee, do you really need to use the bathroom? Now remember you must be truthful. It is only your first day here, I would hate for things to get ugly so soon.

Chapter 6
Follow The Rules

SINCE THIS IS YOUR new home; at least for now, you need to know all of the rules. Rule number one, you will ask every time you want something or want to do something. If I say no then you must obey, no questions asked. If you question my decision, you will be punished. Rule number two, don't lie to me. I just need for you to be honest with me, that shouldn't be difficult. I know how much you love honesty, so that should be the easiest rule for you to follow. Rule number three, you will be allowed to leave the house but only when that thing on your wrist there glows green. It will only allow you to go on my property, no further than that. If you try to go past my property line, that watch there will send a signal to your brain that will cause you to faint. When you are unconscious, I will do with you as I please. So I think that it would be in your best interest to not test it to see what will happen. These are all of the main rules. You will not be caged in one room or just one part of the house. What's mine is yours, and you are free to roam most of the time. You are not here to be my pet, and you are not here to entertain me. "Then why Ara, why am I here? Why wont you let me just go home? Can you answer me that?" I owe you nothing, I don't have to tell you anything at all. I only have to tell you what I please. For now all I want to share are the rules, I don't want to see you hurt. "Okay, I will try to play by the rules. I'll be good, I won't disappoint you. So since I'm here, can we still have movie night? I mean what else is there for us to do?" Cherokee says. Movie night, are you dumb? NO we will not have a movie night, there never was a movie night. I needed you to trust me, and gaining your trust was easier than I could ever have even imagined. I needed you to fall in love with me, because I know that now you have a weak spot for me. I know that the circumstances have changed, but deep down you still care for me. Deep down I am still your Romeo. I am still on that pedestal that you put me on in that pretty little head of yours. You see, there was a reason I chose you. It wasn't just because of your beauty, although that did have a lot to do with it. It was your charisma, it was the insecurity that was emitting off of you. It was the abandonment issues that I could smell from a mile away. I knew that you wouldn't resist me, and I knew that when this day would come things would go according to plan. "What is your plan?" Cherokee says with concern. Oh well its quite simple actually. I wanted to be able to hold you captive, without you feeling like you are being held captive. Deep down I know that you aren't really scared. Apart of you feels secure, and like a weight has been lifted off your shoulders. You still love me, and you are happy that we will be together all the time. Because now you don't have to worry about me leaving you, there is no question about that. And I needed that, I needed someone that deep down would enjoy this. I didn't want someone that would be acting out and crying every day missing mommy and daddy. I know that you will be just fine here, and you know it. The only part of you that is actually concerned about this is so small that it barely even exists. You are happy about this, admit it. "Happy about being a prisoner? You really believe that I am happy that the person that I thought I was in love with turned out to be someone completely different? Someone who is completely insane, someone who is claiming to not even be human? You really think I'm not afraid? You are wrong, you are so wrong. It just goes to show how little you really know me, and that is really disappointing. You don't think I'm scared? You don't think I'm questioning who you are, if you aren't human then what are you? Do you have a second face? Maybe tentacles? Maybe killer spit? Who knows, well I guess you do. But I am frightened, I am terrified actually. But most of all, right now I'm mad. I'm so mad at myself, I cant believe I didn't see the signs. I should have known that there was something off about you, I shouldn't have shrugged off those feelings when I did start to feel like something could be off. But I doubted myself, and I should have never done that. I'm terrified of you, and I'm mad at myself. So no, I'm not happy about this. I am not happy that I am now being held captive and will probably never see the outside world again. I'll never get to spend the day in Barnes and Noble again. I'll never get to try the new Starbucks drinks that will come out. Ill never see any new movies, I'm stuck. I don't feel happy about that, I can't believe you are really that delusional." Cherokee says. "Really, that's really how you feel? I suppose I can see some truth in that, but you aren't telling the whole truth. You are leaving things out, and you know it. Be honest with me, be completely honest with me, tell me how you feel. Tell me the truth, the whole truth. " I just told you, but I guess you are right. I guess there is more to it, but I wasn't lying. I don't feel happy but I do feel something. I don't really know what to call it, but there is a feeling deep down inside of me. It feels content, almost like I deserve this somehow. I deserve whatever is to come. I don't know what your intentions are, and if you plan to hurt me. But I assume you don't plan on letting me go, and this is where ill be spending the rest of my life. I know that I feel relieved that now I don't have to worry about having any responsibilities. I don't have to worry about anything really, except for staying alive. I don't know if I still love you, but a part of me is happy that now I know that you'll never leave. I know that you'll be in my life forever one way or another, and I feel good about that. I know that its probably wrong, but I cant help how I feel." Cherokee, I'm going to ask you something. Please don't lie to me, please don't make me do things that I don't want to do. Do you still love me? Be honest. Ara says. "Jack. I'm sorry Ara, I don't know. I don't know if I still love you because I don't even know who you are. Our whole relationship was built on a lie, and you pretended to be someone that you aren't. You put on a performance, and I don't know who you are. You had ulterior motives the entire duration of our relationship. A girl Is always afraid of being cheated on, or having a secret family. That is usually what a girl thinks of, who would ever think that this would be the worst that could happen? I know I would have never seen this coming. I just thought that maybe there could have been someone else. But you have an entire world that I knew nothing about, and I can see it in your eyes that you expect me to be okay with it. You want me to tell you that I still love you. You believe that I still love you. You believe that this wont change anything, and that in some twisted way that we can still be a couple. But I'm sorry to tell you that isn't the case, that's not what's going to happen. The minute you put this bracelet on me was the minute that we ceased being a couple. I cant sit here and lie to you and tell you that I still feel the same way about you. I Know that isn't what you want to hear or believe, so ill probably get punished. But that's the truth, I don't still feel the same way. Right now I am frightened, do you understand that? How can I still love you and be afraid of you at the same time Ara? I cant, that just doesn't work." Is that your final answer?" Ara says with a blank stare. "Yes, that's my final answer. I don't feel the same, I don't love you. I'm sorry."

Ara grabs Cherokee by her hair and drags her into the basement. He didn't want to accept that he could be wrong. He thought that they had created an unbreakable bond. The bond is broken, and Ara cant accept that. Ara felt deep down that she would change her mind, but in that moment he didn't care. In that moment he became very angry, and he couldn't see anything but anger clouding his mind. Ara straps Cherokee to a chair in the basement to prevent her from moving. "Here's what's going to happen, I am going to rip your finger nails off one by one. You are not going to scream, and you are not going to cry. You are going to sit here and take it, and you are going to think about what you just said to me. Do you understand?"

Yes, I understand." Cherokee whimpers. "Good girl."

Ara takes a pair of plyers out of his pocket that he swiped from the kitchen on his way down to the basement. He looks at the plyers, then looks up at Cherokee. He opens the plyers and places it on the edge of her index finger nail. He closes them with force and rips upwards to peel the nail from the nail bed.

The nub of flesh now visible, is gushing blood. Cherokee is in agony and wants to cry, but she doesn't want to make the situation worse. At this point she has no idea what this man is truly capable of, and she didn't want to find out. Tears rolled down her rosy cheeks, but she didn't make a sound. Her eyes turning red from trying with all of her energy to hold in her screams of pain. The room filled with red, and Ara looks satisfied. He looks like he is enjoying every moment. He takes her pulsating bleeding finger and puts it in his mouth. Cherokee wants to ask what he's doing; but she knows that if she opens her mouth In this moment to try to speak, only screams will escape. Ara is sucking the blood from Cherokees finger. She says nothing, and he keeps sucking. "You taste wonderful, did you know that? God I love how you taste, I bet other parts of you taste even better. How come we were never intimate? Are you a virgin?" Cherokee bites down on her lip and takes a deep breath. Tears still streaming down her bright red face, she knew she had to answer him. "Yes, but that's not why. I just wasn't ready, I like to...take things slow." Cherokee has a hard time getting her sentence out because she wants to scream from the excruciating pain. "You like to take things slow huh, well now that you are here with me there is no need for that. We can do any and everything together. I think we should do it." Cherokee has a blank look on her face. "How can you even think about that right now?" Hey watch your tone, I don't like how you are talking to me. I was just thinking about how good your blood tastes, and it made me think of how your other parts taste. Its all connected, all of your parts. But its okay, we don't have to now. But we will, believe me honey we will."

CHEROKEE IS SO FRIGHTENED in this moment, the true monster within her boyfriend has come to light.

She felt that the only thing that she could do would be apologize. "I'm sorry for earlier, I really am sorry." Do you really mean that? Ara says. "Yes, I do. I am sorry, I do still love you. I just think that we will need some time to adjust to our new life, that's all. You can understand that, cant you?" Oh baby I understand, I love you too. Ara leans over to kiss Cherokee with blood dripping from his mouth. "How about I try to make it up to you, ill cook for you. Out of all of the time we've spent together, you've never tried my famous spaghetti. I make the best spaghetti in the world, I'll prove it to you. How does that sound?" You are going to cook for me, really? That sounds lovely, ill show you where the pots are. Let me untie you so we can walk upstairs, there is no need for all of this. I hope that you learned your lesson, so that way you don't have to come back down here.

Ara unstraps Cherokee and walks her upstairs to the kitchen. He shows her where everything is that she will need to cook. Cherokee fills up a pot with water from the sink and walks it over to the stove. She prepares her vegetables while the water boils.

Once the water comes to a boil, she turns off the stove. Ara asks why she did that before putting the pasta in it, but she didn't say anything. Cherokee picks up the pot, and splashes the boiling water on Ara. She tries to run, but trips over the rug beneath her feet. Ara grabs her by her hair and drags her back down to the basement. "Didn't I tell you that you cant escape? Even if you didn't trip you can not leave my property, so dumb of you to try something so silly. Now you've really made me mad." Ara throws her across the room and locks the door behind him. He stomps up the stairs and grabs his car keys. Ara goes back to the mall where he first met Cherokee. He was now in the mood to kill, and he knew exactly who he wanted. Ara loved the way Cherokee looked already, but he felt that she'd look better with long red hair. Ara arrives at the mall and parks his car. He waits in his car until the sun starts to go down. Once most of the cars in the parking lot left, he got out of his car and walked into Macys. He walks to the beauty section and asks for Gloria. The beauty clerk that was at the counter said that she was on break, but she'd be back soon. Ara walked around trying to find her, but he didn't see her anywhere. Then it crossed his mind that she may be a smoker, so she could be outside taking a smoke break. He walks outside near the dumpsters, and there she was. Sucking down her cancer stick, but Ara didn't judge. He'd never tried smoking himself, but he always wondered what it was like. "Oh my goodness, well if it isn't Gorgeous Gloria!" Ara says. Do I know you? "You don't remember me? You helped me pick out a little outfit and gave me the suggestion to dye my hair this color about two months ago" Oh I remember you now, Timothy right? What are you doing back here? "Well I was looking for you actually, I wanted some more advice. But I see you are on your break here, do you have an extra one of those?" What? Oh a cigarette, sure help yourself. "Thanks, I wanted to come and properly thank you. I know I should have come sooner, but better late then never at all. Today is my second month anniversary with my girlfriend, I met her right after I left you! Can you believe it?"

Wow, that is amazing. I'm so glad that I could help, love is such a beautiful thing. "It really is isn't it, how is your special guy?" Oh Doug, he is great. He just got a promotion at work, so he's happy about that. I'm glad I could help you. "I'm happy to hear about that, hey I got you a thank you gift actually. Your coworker helped me pick it out. Its in my car, if you wanted to walk over with me I can give it to you. I think you'll love it, its just right over here." Oh thanks but, I really should be going now, my break was over five minutes ago." Oh Gloria, it will only take a second, just walk over with me! I know you are going to love it.

Gloria puts out her cigarette and walks over to Aras car. Ara opens the back door and grabs his pocket knife out of his back pocket, and stabs her repeatedly . "I have always had a thing for red heads." Ara says while taking his last stab into glorias face.

Chapter 7
Human Design

ARA DID FEEL REMORSE in a way for what he did to Gloria. He knew that killing was wrong, but he liked it. In fact he loved to kill, regardless of if its right or wrong. Ara always felt superior, like he was better than everyone else Deep down he always wished that he was human, he felt that would make him perfect. Becoming human would be the ultimate ego stroke for Ara, and he was determined to make it happen. He studied for years the ancient inner earth technology and secrets. He believed that he could achieve becoming a human. Never fully believing in himself prevented him from truly pursuing it, but things have been different lately.

He dragged Glorias lifeless corpse inside of his home and into the basement. He didn't want to look at the corpse for much longer, he didn't know what he might do to it. He threw the lifeless corpse into the room with Cherokee. "I made a mess, I need for you to clean it up." Ara says. "It? This is a woman, this is not an object. This is not something that you just toss away. Did you do this? Did you kill her?" Did I kill her? Of course I killed her, why else would I have a dead body.

What do you think I just found her laying on the ground and decided to take her home with me? Have some sense Cherokee. I am perfectly aware that she is a woman, I knew this woman. But she is no longer a woman, this is a corpse. Therefor, clean IT up. I need you to bathe it. It needs to be cleaned, and I don't want to do it. I get weird around dead bodies, I don't really know how to behave." Ara says. "Why did you kill someone that you know? You said dead bodies, as in plural. Are you around dead bodies a lot? Are you killing woman that you know a lot?" Cherokee pauses. "Are..are you going to kill me?" Do as I say, remember I don't like to repeat myself. I make the rules and you do as I say. I told you to clean up this body. I didn't come down here for you to question me. I don't mean to be harsh, I do love you and you know that. I just don't feel in the mood to be interrogated, I did just kill someone after all. If I feel like sharing my reasoning, then I will do so. I will do so on my own time and when I feel good and ready. I'm not going to answer just because you ask, you don't run the show here. Got it? "I understand, I'm sorry for making you repeat yourself. Ill take care of this right away, ill yell to you when I am finished."

Cherokee stares at the lifeless corpse in front of her with curiosity. She wondered who this woman was, and how she ended up dead in a basement. She wondered what her life was like, and who she was to Ara. She suspected that this could have been one of Aras lovers. She thought that maybe he had other girls locked up somewhere. Cherokee wondered if she was next. She tried not to let her mind wander, but she was scared. She was scared that she would be next. She didn't want to say anything or ask Ara because she's not supposed to make him repeat himself. Since he already said that he will talk when he's ready, she knew that asking again would only cause trouble. Cherokee gets up and drags the body into the bathroom down the hall. There were no lights and Cherokee felt so uneasy. She was afraid that she may uncover new bodies, since she knew there was so much of Aras home that shed never seen before. She walked quickly dragging the body along, and propped it up when she reached the bathroom door. She felt around with her hand on the wall to try to find the light switch. Once she found it, she was alarmed to see the most well kept bathroom shed ever seen. Ara never talked about his finances, but she felt like there was a possibility that he had inherited a fortune . The old bathroom was converted in a very modernized and feminine way. It would give the impression that he knew that Cherokee would be coming, and he designed the bathroom for her. It made her question how long he had been plotting to bring her there, but it really didn't bother her as much as it should. Cherokee takes the body over to the gigantic bathtub and props it up inside of it. She sees that there is an abundance of soaps and body washes. There are so many brands and scents to choose from, this excited Cherokee. She had never had that many options before, mainly because she never thought to stock up in that way. She felt like maybe Ara would take good care of her, and she'd never have to worry about anything again. She'd never have to worry about the outside world, and that comforted Cherokee. Cherokee had enough money on her own, but what her life lacked most was support. She was always lonely, and she never had anyone in her corner except for Anna. She never had anyone there for her in times of need. Her therapist was paid to talk to her, so she didn't really feel like that was a person that she could really lean on. Anna had a life of her own, Cherokee didn't feel like she would understand her. She felt that there was no need to truly open up to her because she never felt worthy of having Anna as a friend. She went through every battle alone, barely making it through each one. She never felt love, and that took a toll on her. All she has to do from this point moving forward is follow Aras rules, and she'll be set for life. She will be covered financially, and emotionally. Having to clean up a dead body was a little disturbing, but she was okay with it. She talked to the corpse as if it were still a living breathing human. She realized in that moment that everything would be okay, as long as she played her cards right. She bathed Glorias corpse and then called to Ara.

"YOU ARE ALL FINISHED I see" Ara says. "I am, hey did you design this bathroom for me? Its beautiful, its totally my style. "I did, I'm glad that you like it. I was nervous that you wouldn't like it. I thought that you'd hate me for keeping you here, and forcing you to do things that you don't want to do. You know, like bathing a corpse. I thought that you'd be disobedient and that I would have to do bad things. But I'm glad that things are going well, and I'm glad that you like the bathroom. I'm sorry for getting snippy with you and being mean sometimes. I'm not evil you know, I'm really not. There is just so much about my life that you don't know." Honestly I was a little nervous at first. I wont lie to you, I was incredibly nervous. I didn't really know what to make of the situation. I was nervous when you brought down this body because I didn't know if I would be next. But either way, I'm happy. I've had some time to think, and I really am happy here. I'm not just saying that so that way you'll let me go, I don't want to go. I like being here with you, I like knowing that I always have you. I like that. So even if sometimes you present me with tasks that I don't necessarily want to do, I am still happy. And I want you to know that its normal for couples to fight. If we fight it doesn't mean that I hate you, or that my feelings have changed. Every couple goes through things, it is normal. I don't want you to feel like you have to do anything drastic just because we are in a fight, just let things blow over. Cherokee says sincerely. "I'm glad that you are happy here. I know that these circumstances aren't ideal, but things will be okay. We can be happy here together. And if you would like, I can show you more rooms. There are so many rooms, and I think that you love them. In fact, I think that you deserve to see the room that I just finished up for you. If you don't like it you don't have to stay in it, there are plenty others. But I really think that you will like it. But before I show you the room, we just have one more thing to do first." I cant wait to see the room, I'm sure that I will love it. "I appreciate the enthusiasm, help me put the body in this wheel chair."

Ara wheels Gloria down the hall to the room of horrors, also known as Ara's surgical room. He puts the body onto a hospital bed, and puts a cover over it. "So what are we doing in here, I cant really make out the vibe of this room." Cherokee says. "I will need your assistance, will you help me? "Sure, what do you need for me to do?" I need for you to go into the drawer in the corner, and take one of those white pills. Just sit and wait a few minutes, and soon you will sleep. "Um, okay." Do you trust me Cherokee? "I do, I do trust you."

Cherokee walks over to the drawer and pulls out a white pill like Ara asked of her. She took the pill, simply not to cause a fight between them. She was afraid of what he may do to her in her sleep, but she was even more afraid of what he would do if she told him no. She sat In a chair in the corner of the room and waited for the pill to kick in. When she woke up, she was lying on the hospital bed and the corpse was no where in sight. "Rise and shine beautiful, you look so incredible." Ara says. "Beautiful? I just woke up, I don't think I could look that beautiful." Oh but sweetheart you do, you look so beautiful. Ill show you as long as you promise not to freak out. "Freak out? Why would I freak out? What did you do to me while I was sleeping?" Just promise me, promise me you wont freak out. I want us to get along, lets please just get along. So promise me that you wont be mad or anything. "You are right, I want us to get along too. I promise not to freak out."

Ara hands Cherokee a mirror so she can look at her reflection. She stares blankly at the woman staring back at her, unable to recognize her identity. She sees her face, but something is different. She notices that she has someone else's hair on her head, she is wearing Glorias long ginger hair on her head like a wig. Except this was no wig, this was glorias scalp infused to her own. "Ara what did you do? Why do I look like this? What is going on?" Cherokee asks. You are incredibly beautiful Cherokee, and you know that. You know that I think that you are the most beautiful girl in the world right? "Thank you Ara, I know that you feel that way. I don't know if I really feel that way about myself, but I love that you feel that way about me. "It's the truth, I just wanted to make a minor adjustment. Something that I felt that would make you look even more perfect, and something to give you a bit of a confidence boost. Do you like it Cherokee? "Ara I do, I really do. I was startled at first, but I do love it. I feel like all you really had to do was dye my hair, but this is what you chose to do. I wont question or judge your decisions. I do feel more confident, I feel more confident than I've ever felt in my entire life. I don't know if its just because of the new hair, or if its because I've got a great guy that tells me how beautiful I am all the time. Either way, I love it. I love you Ara, I want to be with you for the rest of my life. I don't know how long that will be, but I don't care. I just want to be with you." So are you really telling me the truth? You really love me? You really don't feel like a prisoner here? You were so angry before, I thought that I had lost you. I thought that our bond had been destroyed. I don't know if you just say these things to try to keep yourself safe, but I wouldn't hurt you unless I had to. But you've been good, such a good girl. I don't want to have to hurt you, I just want to love you. "I mean it, I really mean it. I'm happy to be here, and I'm happy to be with you. I want to make love, can we make love? Kiss me Ara." Are you sure? Are you really sure? I don't want you to feel pressured. If you aren't ready we don't have to do anything. "Ara just shut up and kiss me."

Ara leans over to kiss Cherokee. He presses his lips against hers gently. She kisses him back passionately and a tear rolls down her left cheek. "What's wrong, why are you crying?" I love you, I just never imagined our first time being like this. "Our first time being like what?" Ara says confused. "Nothing just kiss me". Ara and Cherokee continue to passionately kiss and Ara rips Cherokees shirt off. "I've never seen you naked before, you are so beautiful Cherokee."

Ara forcefully grabs Cherokees body and pushes her torso down. He pulls her panties off and rubs his hands up her thighs. He graces his fingers over her vagina to tease her. He inserts his middle and ring finger inside of her to feel how warm and wet she was. He looks up to her and smiles. "You are so wet, you like how daddy's fingers feel inside of you huh baby?" Yes, I want you. He takes his fingers in and out and speeds up the pace. "How is that, you like that?" Go deeper. Cherokee moans. Ara sticks his fingers inside of her as deep as he can get them and continues to finger her rapidly. "You want something else inside of you baby?" Yes, I want to feel you inside of me. Cherokee moans. Ara unzips his pants and pulls out his erect penis. Cherokee takes her fingers and plays with her clit in a circular motion. "How bad do you want it?" So bad, I want it so bad. Its so big, I want you inside of me. "I want to watch you play with yourself before I go inside of you. Can you do that for daddy?" Cherokee looks Ara in the eye and rubs her clit faster until she feels like she is about to cum. "Please daddy, I need you." Cherokee moans. Ara takes his penis and slaps it on her clit. "Not yet." Then he slowly sticks his tip in and goes in and out. "You want the whole thing? Tell daddy you want the whole thing. I want to hear you beg for it. "Daddy please, I'm ready for you. Please please fuck me, please daddy please. "That's a good girl". Ara slowly inserts his entire shaft inside of her and begins to pump in and out. "I want you to cum for me, can you cum for daddy." Ara says while aggressively pumping his penis inside of her. "Fuck!!!" Cherokee moans. Cherokee cums on Aras penis and Ara continues pumping. "I'm not finished with you yet baby girl." Ara continues stroking until he is finished. When he finishes he pulls out of her and eats her out. "You taste so good baby." Yeah? Cherokee moans. Ara takes his front teeth and bites down on her clit. "Ow that hurts, don't use your teeth like that."

Ara takes a bite and swallows Cherokees clit. Cherokee screams in agony. "What the hell, why would you do that?!" I can make the pain go away, I can make it come back. Do you want that? You want your clit back? "Do it then." Cherokee struggles to say. "All you have to do is drink from me, drink my blood. The more you drink the faster you heal, and the more effective it will be. "You want me to drink your blood, like some kind of weird vampire shit?" Just do it, I promise it will work. I wouldn't lie to you, just trust me. I wouldn't have done it if I didn't have a way to heal you. Id like to be able to use your clit again you know. So just do it, and watch what happens. "I really don't want to do that, I really don't feel comfortable doing that. I need medical attention, this hurts so bad." Remember I told you that I am not from here? Remember when I told you that I wasn't human? We have special abilities and advanced technology, I can show you all of it If you want. I can show you all that I can do, but if you don't listen to me you wont live to see it. You will bleed out, and you will die. Just do it Cherokee, do it before its too late. "Fine."

Ara takes his finger nail and presses deeply into his wrist until he starts to bleed.

"Your blood, its different." Yes I know, that is what I am trying to tell you. Just drink it please, drink my blood Cherokee. Ara says angrily. Cherokee leans over to Aras gushing wound and begins to drink the blood. She notices that the pain is disappearing and can feel the flesh coming back. She continues to drink until she feels completely normal again.

"That worked, that actually worked." I tried to tell you, aren't you glad that you listened to me now? "Yes, I am. Now I'm curious about the other things that you can do and the technology that you have." Ill share that with you, in due time. Now we are officially bonded, I drank your blood and you drink mine.

Chapter 8

Bon Appetit

ARA WE DIDN'T NEED to drink each others blood to be bonded. We already are bonded, although I would have to say that your blood must be infused with some kind of magic. I don't know if I understand why we always have to go through such drastic measures. Was it really necessary to bite me like that? All just so that way you can show me that you have the ability to heal me with your blood? "It absolutely was necessary, do you really think that I would have done it if it weren't?" Ara I don't know, and that is my point. I understand that you want to tell me things on your own time, I do understand that. I don't want to make you uncomfortable and force you to talk when you aren't ready. But after you do something as drastic as what you just did to me, I think that at this point I deserve some answers. I think that I deserve a lot of answers. I think that it is unfair that I have to follow your rules. We are a couple, a real couple. You shouldn't treat me like a hostage if you don't want me to feel that way. We should be acting like a real couple, don't you think? Don't you think that I deserve some answers?. I'm not asking for you to tell me everything, I just need something. You've got to tell me what Is going on. "Fine; you're right, ill tell you. You get two questions, and that's all I feel comfortable with sharing at this moment. Is that okay with you? Can you accept that, at least just for right now? Ill tell you whatever you want to know, but you only get two questions. So you need to make sure that you choose your questions wisely because I don't know when the next time will be that I feel like opening up." Thank you, ill take it. I appreciate that you are willing to make a compromise, like what real couples do. "You keep saying real couple this real couple that, Cherokee don't you think that we are a real couple? We are a real couple, and its starting to upset me that you keep saying that if I'm being frank with you." Ara you know what I mean. "Actually Cherokee; I don't, I don't know what you mean." Ara you do, and you are just being difficult. Why are you trying to pick a fight with me? After you just did what you did, don't you feel like that's enough? "Oh Cherokee get over it already, you are healed. There is no need to keep whining about it, its over with. Tell me what you mean, I want to know. If you don't tell me then I wont tell you a thing." I thought we were making progress. I thought that we were moving in a healthy direction of being like normal couples. I cant believe I was that dumb to even think such a thing. Ara you know exactly what I am talking about, and I don't know why you are acting like you don't have a clue. You are well aware of the fact that I am here against my will. You asked me to move in with you, and I said no. A normal boyfriend would have just been disappointed, but eventually get over it. But you chose to kidnap me, and keep me here against my will. You know what you did, or did you forget? Nothing about that is normal. Nothing about us is normal. For Gods sake Ara you killed someone, you murdered an innocent human being. Normal boyfriends don't kill people. And when you think that things cant get worse, they do. You bring home the dead body and force your girlfriend to bathe the dead body. Normal couples don't do stuff like that, and you know that Ara. You are not dumb Ara, I know that you are not dumb. I would have never fallen for a dummy, and I fell for you. So please, don't make this more difficult than it needs to be. "I know Cherokee, I just wanted to hear you say it. I knew that you resented me and I knew that you didn't really want to be here. I knew that you felt like I was holding you captive, and you were putting on a show acting like you were still in love with me. Things have changed, so your performance was shit. I just needed to hear you say it." God dammit Ara you are living in your head to much, you need to get out. I am trying to tell you that I want to be like a normal couple. Even though we cant be a normal couple, we can still be *like* a normal couple. And of course a part of me has some resentment towards you, but that doesn't mean that I don't love you. I don't want you to twist my words and hurt your own feelings. "Ask your two questions, your time is running out." Ara says hastily. "We have all the time in the world, there is no need to rush me. I guess my first question would be why did you put me asleep and what happened to the body?" Are you sure you really want to know? I'm not sure if you want to know the answer to that, are you sure there isn't anything else that you want to ask right now? "I asked what I asked, don't shy away from the questions. Be honest with me, tell me as much as possible please Ara." If you insist, I just don't want to scare you. I don't want you to think any less of me, I'm so scared of losing you. I'm so afraid that you are going to stop loving me, especially when you learn about who I really am. I put you to sleep because I did a scalp infusion. I didn't want you to be in pain, and I also didn't want you to see what I did to the corpse. I already gave you a little bit of my blood, but it was only enough to stop your pain from that procedure. I cut the body up, one limb at a time. I skinned the entire body and put all of the parts aside, except for the scalp. I removed your scalp and replaced it with hers. I really don't want to hurt you Cherokee, I really love you. That's why I gave you my blood, so that way it wouldn't hurt. Yes I know that I could have just dyed your hair, that would have been an easier way to do it. I am well aware of that, but I had to make use of the body. While using her body parts, apart of her is now fused into you. Some of her personality traits will begin to emerge from you. That isn't something that can be obtained by a simple bottle of hair dye. After I finished the procedure, I consumed the rest of the body." You...you did what? " I know it may sound a little strange to you, but I had to do it. You know that I am not like you, you know that I'm not human. Well apart of that causes a bit of a difference in diet. Do you understand? " No Ara I don't understand, you still are being vague. Why do you have to be vague?" Fine Cherokee, you win. I really don't feel comfortable talking to you about this because I don't want you to look at me any differently. "I just want to understand, and I just want us to have open communication. You keeping things from me makes me view you differently, so just spit it out. "I am not a vampire, but I do require blood. It is hard for me to drink blood because when my kind drinks the blood of a human, it is the beginning stages of a binding process. I don't like being partially bonded to just anyone. We don't have to eat in the same way humans do. Humans have to eat around three times a day, although a lot of you don't. The point is that you need food more often in order to function. I can go a long time without eating, but when you go a long time without eating it has an effect on you. I have created a synthetic blood using inner earth technology that allows me to not have to feast on human blood. I am sort of famous down there, I changed history. My people don't go up to earth, but for a really long time someone had to go in order to get blood. They called the creatures night walkers, and there one and only purpose in life was to obtain human blood and bring it back down to us. These creatures are very scary looking and we never liked having to send them up to earth, but we had to. That's when I decided to make a change in my community and create something that would change our lives forever. I enjoyed the money and the fame for awhile, for a long while in fact. Eventually I grew bored of that, and wanted to be out of the spot light. I always had this deep desire to meet and study humans. I also really wanted to be a human, that's when I came to earth. I know I am getting a bit off track, but I wanted to give you as much information as I could. I really didn't need to drink anyone's blood, that isn't why I did it. It had nothing to do with the feeding aspect. I ate the body mostly because I wanted to. I also just wanted to keep her close, so she'd live on inside of me. I don't want you to be afraid of me." I appreciate your honesty, I think there is hope for us after all. This is sort of a lot to have to come to terms with, so do you mind giving me some time with my thoughts? Please don't put words into my mouth and say that now I view you differently, don't do that. Because that isn't the case at all. I just simply want some time with my thoughts, don't think too deeply into it. "Do you still love me Cherokee? I never want to loose you, I never want to loose your love."

Don't be silly Ara, of course I still love you. Nothing has changed, we are still us. We are still going to be us as long as you don't do any harm to me. Please don't harm me, I'm trying my best here. "I wont harm you, I love you. I just want us to be happy together." And we will be, don't rush things. Just allow things to flow, okay? "Okay. Ill be right upstairs if you need me. We can talk again whenever you are ready to talk again."

After Ara left, he grew very distant with Cherokee. Whenever she wanted to talk to him or be around him, he was never anywhere to be found. She cooked meals for the both of them, but he never ate with her. She would leave his plate on the stove, and he would come eat it when he heard that she was gone. Cherokee didn't know why Ara was acting this way, but it made her lonely. Cherokee knew deep down that she was being held captive, but on the surface her abandonment issues made her think that she was really still in love with her captor. She truly believed that she was in a healthy loving relationship. She loved Ara unconditionally, the things that he did never really turned her off. Going weeks without seeing or hearing from him made her feel like she was going mad. One day she decided to sit in the kitchen after she cooked and waited all night for him to come down. Aras body didn't require human food, but he enjoyed the taste of her cooking. She knew that he would come down eventually, because eating her food made him feel close to her. She waited for hours and eventually he came to the kitchen in the middle of the night.

"What are you doing in here, why are you still up?" Ara says. "I waited up for you, I wanted to see you. You've been avoiding me for weeks and I miss you. Why are you doing this to me? You leave me all by myself with no one to talk to, I feel like I'm loosing my mind. I want to be with my boyfriend, I want to be with you. "I just needed some time." After weeks of no communication that's all you have to say? "Cherokee what else am I supposed to say? I just needed some time and that is all that there is to it. I told you some really heavy shit, I've never told that to anyone before. I was embarrassed. I didn't know how you would feel about me once you learned more about me." Why didn't you just talk to me? Why didn't you just ask me how it made me feel? Because I would have told you that I still love you. I would have told you that of course that is some heavy shit, but it is okay. I am not judging you, and I am not looking at you any differently. That's what I would have told you. But instead you isolated me. "I'm sorry I didn't mean to make you feel isolated. I was just afraid of what you would say. I was afraid that you would look at me differently. I don't ever want to make you feel that way again. I have an idea, do you trust me?

Chapter 9
The Perfect Vessel

CHEROKEE TRUSTED ARA, she trusted him more than she should have. She had the right to hate him considering everything that's happened, instead she loves and trusts him. Cherokee was comfortable in her conditions, she was comfortable with the chaos always happening around her. She told Ara that she trusted him with every fiber in her body, he took that and ran with it. Ara goes to the local coffee shop in town called Café Gattivi to observe. Ara went to Café Gattivi whenever he got in a fight with Cherokee. The café was his safe haven, he didn't feel like he had to pretend to be someone that he wasn't. The staff knew him as Elijah, but he never portrayed new personality traits each visit. In the café he wasn't "weird Ara" he was just Elijah. Ara ordered his favorite drink, an iced matcha latte blended with hot chocolate. He got this drink every time, and every time the staff always asked him if it really was good. He chuckled each time and told him that they should try it. No one ever tried it, until this day. Ara took his drink and sat in the seat near the window. He watched the raindrops fall from the awning and drop on the mini outdoor seating table. No one usually sits out there, its too secluded. Café Gattivi attract-ed a lot of frivolous and free spirited people. Normal people don't usually go there, and Ara liked that. He liked that he nev-er felt out of place, because everyone there was strange. Every-one came to take a deep breath ,without feeling the judgment from the outside world. The staff is unusually kind to every-one, even the people who didn't seem deserving of such kind-ness. Perverts loved to hang out and just stare at the young girls. Ara hated perverts, but in this setting he didn't mind their pres-ence around him. Ara knew that he wasn't normal, he knew that he had skeletons in his closet. He tried not to judge, but the thoughts did slip through sometimes. The same way that his raging homicidal thoughts slipped through. Ara didn't feel out of place and odd due to his homicidal thoughts. He felt that those were normal. Not normal in the way that everyone else had them, but normal in the way that he just simply didn't care enough to feel weird about it. Its just apart of who he is, and he had no real desire to change.

He watched the rain hit the table outside and thought about what he should do. He felt awful that he made Cherokee feel isolated. He wanted her to feel loved, and nothing less. He felt that the only way to make up for making her feel that way was to do something big. Aras mind didn't work the same way as everyone else's. Most couples get into a fight and the boyfriend buys his girlfriend an "I'm sorry" necklace or some kind of jewelry. The girl gets so distracted by the sparkle, that she completely forgets how bad he made her feel. They kiss and make up and everything is fine. Ara is not like everyone else, he's not even human. Ara's idea of a big gesture is always some-thing out of the ordinary.

THE PERFECT VESSEL

His first instinct was to remove his heart and gift it to her in a flashy diamond box, he didn't really need it. He needed a heart, but he didn't need the heart that was in his body. He decided against this gesture because he didn't know what she would do with a human heart. Of course it was the gesture which would have made it special, but there is nothing that she could do with it. He thought that maybe he could teach her how to use inner earth technology, maybe even bring her to his home. Humans have never been to the part that he resides in, she would make history. Shed be famous, especially with Aras status. What pretty girl doesn't want to be rich and famous? She could live the life of her dreams, she could live the life that he deserved. Ara didn't want to do this because his ultimate plan was to kill her. He never intended for her to have much of a future. If they were in the spotlight, everyone would know. Everyone would know that Ara was a killer, everyone would look at him differently. Ara was deeply afraid of being judged, he was always worried about what people thought of him. This was apart of the reason he never wanted to stick to one personality. If someone didn't like him, all he had to do was just become someone else. Ara knew that he couldn't merge Cherokees world with his own. That wouldn't end well for anyone. After going back and forth with himself about finding the right gesture, a miracle happened. A beautiful blonde walks over to him and sits in the chair across from him. Ara really felt like Cherokee was the most beautiful girl in the world, nothing could ever change that. There was something about this blonde barista that intrigued Ara. She had a promiscuous stride in her walk, and a sensual quality to the way that she carried herself. She wasn't intentionally trying to be sexy, she just had an undeniable erotic nature. Ara noticed her before, but she never took his order. He noticed how she kept to herself while emitting this animalistic sexual energy. She made people feel nervous just by looking at her. She was intimidating in the way that she knew she was capable of making all of your deepest fantasies come to life with little effort. She had a goddess energy that reeled people in, but not allowing them to feel comfortable enough to approach her. She looked like she'd do anything in bed, but no one would ever have the opportunity to explore her in that way. She was a tease, and she didn't even have to lift a finger to make you have a waking wet dream. Ara didn't know why someone like this would talk to him. Girls that powerful and sexy never approached him. This made Ara hungry for her, he wanted her.

"WHAT'S GOT YOU TROUBLED on this dismal day?" Dismal? I love this kind of weather. Ara says. "Do you really? Are you a dreary kind of guy?" No, at least I don't think that I am. "Well then, what kind of guy are you?" I don't really know. I mean I guess I know who I am. Sometimes I just feel a little lost. This weather soothes me, I love the rain. I think its relaxing. "I agree, rain is relaxing. Especially on days where your troubles get the best of you. I can't say that I like rainy days on most occasions, but I do like the rain when something has got me down. So mister, has something got you down?" I suppose, but I'm fine. "You can talk to me if you want to, I hear that I'm a pretty good listener. I'm a pretty good problem solver too, well except for when it comes to my own problems." Are you sure? You don't even know me. "I'm sorry, where are my manners? I'm Alice, and you?" I'm...Elijah...Well Ara. Its complicated. "Nice to meet you Elijah...Ara. Now we know each other." If only it were really that simple. "Why cant It be that simple? Just let It be that simple. If I can help you with whatever is troubling you, that'll only bring us closer." Closer? We aren't close at all, we just met. "Well maybe we should get close, would that be such a bad thing?" Ara looks down into his beverage with hesitation.

"I guess not, you are really pretty. I know that you know that. Its very obvious in the way that you move that you know that." I do know that. Alice smirks. "Good, I like that you know that. There are a lot of pretty girls in the world that don't know how beautiful they are and they don't like themselves. They ought to, they ought to know how special they are." Do you think I'm special? " No I don't think that you are special. You are special, there is no doubt about that. You are undeniably...special." Are you saying that I'm special because I'm pretty? "I'm saying that you're special because you are special, your beauty Is a bonus." But you don't even know me. "I thought we knew each other?" Alice chuckles.

Okay I see your point, but you are right. I am special. So tell me Elijah...Ara what has you troubled? "I have a girlfriend" And that has you troubled? "No...well yes. But I just had to tell you because I just told you that you are pretty."

Are you not allowed to tell other girls that they are pretty? "I don't know, I just needed to inform you. I did something bad but I don't feel bad about it. I ended up dragging my girlfriend into my mess and I got scared that she would view me differently. She wanted me to tell her some really personal things, things that I never wanted for her to know. The type of things that no one should know. I had to tell her because I owed her that. I owed her some truth because of the mess that I dragged her into. After I told her about my personal things I felt so embarrassed. I couldn't bare the idea of her looking me in the eye and having to wonder if she is viewing me differently. I avoided her, for awhile. Avoiding her only made matters worse and it made her feel isolated. I never wanted her to feel isolated. I didn't want to make her feel lonely. We live together and she doesn't really leave the house so I'm really all that she has. She has no one else and I abandoned her. I feel so awful that I made her feel that way all because I was afraid to face her. "I'm sure that you are just being hard on yourself. You seem like a nice guy, so I'm sure what you did wasn't that bad. Your past is your past and there is nothing that you can do to change that. So whatever you told her probably wasn't as bad as you think. You cant beat yourself up over it. You have to allow for things to just happen. Since you feel bad, that's a good sign. That means that you aren't a sociopath, and that's something. You have to just try a little harder to find some sort of positivity, even when it feels like there isn't any. You've taken responsibility and that's something too. The little things add up, and they matter. I think that you should do something nice for her, show her that you are sorry." You are right, and I really appreciate you saying that. The little things do matter, no one Is perfect. I am really hard on myself. I want to make it up to her, I really do. That's what I was thinking about before you sat down. I just cant seem to think of the perfect gesture or gift. Nothing that I think of is good enough. I feel like I'm not even good enough. I'm not good enough for her. "And yet you are with her. She feels like you are good enough for her. You have to just think a little bigger, and try a little harder. That's all you have to do. Maybe I can help you." How can you help me? I don't think anyone can help with this. "Oh but you are so wrong. I can help you, in fact if you let me I will help you. Will you let me help you?" Why would you want to do that? We just met, you don't owe me anything. "I know I don't owe you anything, other than basic human decency. But I want to help you. You have this look in your eye of desperation. That's why I came over here. I've never seen someone with such deep desperation in their eyes. You seem like you need me. I can help, I really can. I don't have much going on in my life, so maybe a part of me needs you too Elijah..Ara. And what's with that? Having two names I mean." I've always felt like an Elijah so, I wanted to be an Elijah. But my name is Ara, not Elijah. "That's fascinating. What does an Elijah feel like? And if you like that name so much, why not just get it changed. You can get your name legally changed." Elijah feels free, like nothing really matters. Elijah feels like someone that people don't judge, because Elijah doesn't judge himself. Elijah feels like the person that I want to be, like the person that I'm aiming to be. When I come here, that's what I feel like. "Ill call you Elijah. I don't have to call you by your real name if you don't want me to. I appreciate your honesty, I bet that's something that your girlfriend loves about you. Most guys are such liars, they operate is if telling the truth would cause an allergic reaction. I bet she likes that about you, I know I like that about you. "Thanks, there is something about you Alice. Something that makes me feel like you are a good person to have in your corner." Ill be in your corner, if you want me to of course. This isn't really like me, I feel like I'm throwing myself at you. I'm not usually like this I swear, but I guess that's just who I am today. So Elijah, will you let me help you? Just say yes, I promise you wont regret it. "What are you thinking? How do you think that you can help me?" How far do you live from here? "I live a little far, I make the commute because this place is like my safe haven. I don't really even have any coffee shops that are actually close by. Why do you ask? "I was thinking that you could let me come over? As long as you are really as nice as you seem and you aren't some kind of wierdo. Are you some kind of wierdo Elijah?

Ara chuckles and shrugs his shoulders. "I don't think so, I know that I don't want to be." That's good enough for me. I was thinking I could be friends with you and your girlfriend. Do you think that she'd like that? "I guess that would be good for her, she hasn't seen another person but me in such a long time. Maybe that would help, maybe she should have a friend. "I was thinking that the three of us could be friends. You think I'm pretty, and I think you are cute." What exactly do you mean by that? I don't want to misinterpret you. "You know, the three of us could get together and have a little fun. Friends have fun. So lets all have fun together." What kind of fun, what exactly did you have in mind? "The three of us could get close, really close. So close that we might slip up and-" Oh, that fun. I've never had fun like that before, I don't know how shed feel about it. "I'm sure she'd open up to it, most girls are curious in that way. Most girls fantasize about it, they just don't want to risk getting jealous. I'm not looking for anything serious, so she'd have nothing to worry about. I just want to have a good time. I haven't had a good time with anyone In such a long time." I guess if you think that she'd be okay with it then I'm okay with it "Okay with it? *You are just okay with it?*" Alice mocks. I guess I'd be a little more okay with it, if I'm being honest. "Don't you want me? I know you want me. Don't fight it, its okay. Your girlfriend will love it and we will all have a good time. It'll be a win win for everyone, just think about it." Alice says enthusiastically.

"Lets do it, lets have some fun. You are so pretty." I know.

Alice and Ara leave the café and he drives her to his house. Ara loved Cherokee and thought that she was the one. But now that he's met Alice, he is starting to question everything.

Ara knew that regardless of the outcome, things would never be the same with Cherokee again. Things were changing, and he was okay with it. Ara walks Alice into the front door, she has no idea what she Is walking into. "Your house is so unique, how did you land something like this?" I have a lot of money, more money than anyone should have. I love it though, I love having a lot of money. "Yeah I bet, this is incredible." Oh you ain't seen nothing yet. Ara chuckles. "My place is huge, I won't bore you with a tour right now. I can show you if you want, but I want you to meet my girlfriend first." Oh okay, I bet shell be so shocked. "Follow me, it's just down this way." Oh, are you sure? She's really down there? I don't know, can't she just come up here with us? Can't you just call her? "I could but this way you'll get to see her room. Maybe it'll make you want to stay with her. "Stay with her? This is just a one time thing, I really shouldn't stay." Just follow me, It's okay. "I guess, I just hope this wasn't some tactic to lure me to your house so you can kidnap me. You aren't going to kidnap me, are you Elijah?" You sound paranoid, I thought we knew each other. Just come on, this was your idea anyway. How could I have plotted to kidnap you when you are the one that approached me, and this was all your idea? Don't be silly, everything is fine. I bet you are going to love her. "As long as you promise that you'll take me back to my car before the sun goes down. Can you promise me that?" Sure.

Ara walks Alice into the basement to Cherokees room. Alice is nervous, but she wanted to be fearless. She wanted to do something that she doesn't usually do. Her best friend told her before her shift that she is predictable, and she should loosen up a little. Alice was determined to prove her friend wrong. Despite her fear, she knew that it was too late to turn back now. Alice walked into the bright pink room to see a red-haired girl laying on a California king bed. "Hi, I'm Alice, I love your room." Thanks, what are you doing here? "I met your boyfriend earlier at the café that I work at. He seemed really sad, so I went over to talk to him to try to cheer him up. Do you know why he's sad?" I don't know. That still doesn't answer my question, why are you here? "Well, I proposed to him that maybe we can try to have some fun together. I thought maybe it could cheer us all up, to have some new friends and have some fun together." He brought you here? Someone that he just met, so that way we can 'have fun' together? "It was my idea; I could use the company. Couldn't you use the company Cherokee? Cherokee right?" Yeah, I'm Cherokee. I guess I could use the company but why would you go home with some stranger. He could be a killer. He could kill you. I could kill you, couldn't I? "Well, are you going to kill me?" I don't know, do I have a reason to? "Oh, you're funny, I like you." You just met me. "Yeah, yeah I already had this same conversation with Ara."

THE PERFECT VESSEL

You know his name? He told you his real name? We dated for months before he told me his real name. He didn't tell me until... "Until what?" Until I started living here. "He seemed like he was tired of being someone that he wasn't, he just wanted to be himself for a change." Be himself? You talk like you know him, like you really know him. You don't know anything about him, you don't know who he really is. "Is that necessary? For me to know who he *really* is? I just wanted to have some fun. I don't need to know who he really is at the core. I know enough." You really think that don't you? "You don't like me. Why don't you like me?" I don't know you, Alice, is it? "Yes, Alice. Why not get to know me? I'm here so why not get to know each other? Maybe you'll like me, who knows maybe you'll even love me." I doubt that. "Can we at least try? Let's try to see if we like each other before coming to any conclusions." You are awfully chipper; I don't like that. It's not appropriate, not here. "You need to loosen up a little, get that stick out of your ass. Just relax, there is no need to be so uptight like this. I think you are really pretty; I want to see you in a different way." What do you mean by that? Cherokee barks. "All I'm trying to say is that you'd look better if you were a little looser." Looser? "Yeah, looser. Have you ever been with a girl before?" What like lesbian shit? I'm not a lesbian, I have a boyfriend. "I know that you aren't a lesbian, your boyfriend is the reason that I'm here.

I really want to kiss you; would it be okay if I kissed you? I'm not a lesbian either, I just want to have a little fun." I haven't had any real fun in a while. I just pretty much stay in this room, why not. "Come close." Cherokee leans in hesitantly. "Closer." Cherokee leans into Alice and presses her lips against Alices.

They share an apprehensive lingering closed mouth kiss. Ara walks into the dimly lit bedroom and watches the two beauties settle into each other's bodies. Alice pulls Cherokees black tank top up over her head while still trying to maintain a passionate kiss. She admires Cherokees perfectly shaped breasts while removing her own top. "You have really great tits" Alice says. She leans into Cherokees hard nipples and sucks on them until Cherokee moves her head off of her bosom. "Can I taste you?" Alice says. "Yeah, never had it done by a girl before." It's okay, you'll like it. Alice goes down on Cherokee while Ara approaches the bed. "Join us." Alice moans. Ara unzips his pants and lets them fall down to his ankles. He takes his right hand and rubs on Alice's now exposed vagina. "It's your turn to have fun, fuck me like you fuck Cherokee." Is this, okay? Ara asks Cherokee. "Yeah" Cherokee moans. Ara inserts his pulsating erection inside of Alice and strokes slowly. He enjoys watching the girls play with each other. Alice's middle finger deep inside of Cherokees vagina while flicking her clit with her tongue simultaneously. Ara starts to speed up the pace of his strokes as Alice's vagina gets wetter. "You like this don't you? This is what you wanted you little slut. "Yeah" Alice moans into Cherokees vagina. Ara grabs the back of Alice's neck and chokes her from behind "Look at me while I'm fucking you. I want to see those eyes as my dick stretches this pussy out. You can't leave here until I cum so let me see you make me cum." Alice pushes her butt back to the rhythm of Ara's strokes. "That's a good fucking girl" Ara says while looking into Cherokees eyes. "Roll over, I want to get a better look at you." Alice flips over while Cherokee moves to the side. Ara focuses his attention on Alice, which gives Cherokee the impression that he just wanted to be with someone else. Cherokee no longer feels included because at this point she is just watching her boyfriend plow some strange woman. Cherokee tries, to involve herself but every time she tries her attempts fail. They continue to brush her off and treat her like an outsider. Cherokee starts feeling isolated again, the way she felt before all of this even happened. A tear falls from her eye on to her rosy cheeks. Ara notices that she is crying and pulls out of Alice. "Baby what's wrong? Why are you crying? I thought we were having fun here?" You're having fun, you're having a little too much fun. "We are supposed to be having fun, that's the point." Well, I'm not having fun, I don't want to do this. "It's okay, we don't have to do this."

Ara and Cherokee bicker while the three of them remain unclothed. Alice says that she thinks it's time to go and asks Ara to drive her home. Ara refuses to take her anywhere and tells her that if she doesn't keep her mouth shut then she will never go home. "I did my part, it's not my fault that she can't handle a little fun. It's time for me to go now and you guys can fight in private. This really is none of my business and I should have never gotten involved. "You are right, you should have never gotten involved." Cherokee barks. I was just trying to do something nice for you Cherokee. I wanted to show you that I was sorry. "You wanted to show me that you're sorry by screwing another girl in front of me? How delusional can you be? She tricked you! She got into your head and made you think that this was a good idea. She just wanted this for her own selfish reasons, it was never about me. Can't you see that?" Can't you see that I was just trying to make things right with you? You can't be mad at me for trying! What do you want me to do? Just tell me what you want me to do and I'll do it." Get rid of her. I can't do that, she can't leave here now. You knew that the minute you laid eyes on her. "I didn't mean take her back, I mean get rid of her." I thought that was bad, I thought you wanted to be like normal couples. "I don't care about normal, I just want you to get rid of her. You want to fix things so badly? Then do it. "You guys are scaring me, please don't hurt me."

Alice cries. It's okay, it'll all be over soon. I appreciate you trying to help me but unfortunately it just didn't work. I said that I wouldn't, I knew that it wouldn't.

Ara grabs Alice's neck and squeezes it tightly until he hears it snap. He stares at the body realizing what he had done. "How do you feel?" Cherokee asks. I feel good, are you happy now? "I am. What's next? Are you going to dismember her body like what you did to Glorias?" Not quite. "Then what are you going to do with her?" Cherokee asks. Ara looks Cherokee deep in her eyes and then takes a bite of Alices pointer finger. He looks Cherokee in her eyes while he chews the flesh off of Alices boney fingers until all her fingers are completely consumed. Ara consumed Alices body from head to toe and made Cherokee watch.

"Is this what you wanted?" Ara repeats as he finishes consuming Alices nearly depleted corpse.

"This isn't what I meant, why did you have to do this to her?" She's gone now, I think that we need to get closer. Because your time is approaching, and I need to ensure that you are prepared. "Get closer, what do you mean?" I'm not going to explain right now, all you need to know is that it is important. Drink from me.

Cherokee sinks her teeth into Aras flesh without questioning. He wraps his hands around her left thigh, twisting it until her leg is completely disconnected from her body. Cherokee feels no pain but her leg gushes blood all over her pink décor. Cherokee feels no pain but feels herself slipping away. Her spirit rising out of her body while she watches him consume her dismembered leg. Ara chows down on Cherokees flesh as it were a turkey leg at the renaissance festival. This was normalcy to Ara and felt no remorse for ending the life of his girlfriend. Cherokee hovers over her body looking through it as if she were looking through an Xray. She notices something different about her body, something that was never there before. She gets closer to the abnormality when she realizes what exactly she's looking at. She is so close to her body that her spirit becomes one with her body once again. Cherokee gasps for air and shrieks *IM PREGNANT*!

Chapter 10
The Merge

A CONFUSED CHEROKEE watches her missing limb grow back out of thin air, like pulling a rabbit out of a magician's hat. Terror filled her lungs completely with each gasping breath she screeched. Scared of her fate, discovering the new life growing inside of her. Cherokee whimpers while a frozen Ara gazes into nothingness. The two of them in complete shock, neither of which know how to proceed. Cherokee completely aware of the fact that she died and came back to life. This was shocking, but not as shocking as watching a new limb emerge from her nub. A pregnancy could be good for her, so she thought. The possibility of having someone else other than Ara gave her a sense of ease. Cherokee was lonely, Ara wasn't enough. But she wondered what a life like this would mean for her child.

Being stuck in a house unable to leave and mingle with other humans was lonely. A baby could be perfect, a baby could save her. At least that's what she was thinking while her leg finished developing. "Ara say something." I don't know what to say, how do you know? I can get you a test, there is no way that you know for certain. "I know, trust me I know. There is a life growing inside of me, and its ours. We have a baby, or at least we will have a baby." Just take a test for me, just to confirm. I'll run out to get one. "Ara, I saw it, I saw our baby growing inside of me. I died; you killed me. I left my body and I saw the fetus, I felt the fetus. There is life growing inside of me. I couldn't feel it before I died, but now I feel it. We are going to be parents. Are you ready to be a dad?" I don't know Cherokee, I never imagined being a parent. I didn't even know that I could get someone pregnant. This wasn't a part of the plan; you are ruining the plan. You are ruining everything. "What plan? What are you talking about? I didn't ruin anything, why would you say that? Can you try not to pick a fight with me, not now. "I am not trying to pick a fight with you. Your body will be ruined, what am I supposed to do with it then? "What do you mean by that? My body will go through changes of course, that happens with every pregnancy." You don't understand, you don't know everything. "What don't I know? Maybe if you talked to me more than I would know. You choose to keep so much from me and I'll never understand that." I AM TRYING TO PROC-TECT YOU! YOU DIDN'T NEED TO KNOW EVERY-THING FOR CHRISTS SAKE CHEROKEE. Ara screams. "I am pregnant Ara, do not scream at me. Talk to me like a civilized person. Talk to me like a normal person." You just love to do that don't you? You love to throw in the word. You do it to hurt me. You know how I feel about myself. Imagine how I feel. I am not human, yet I am living in a world full of them. No matter what I do, I will never be normal. You love to throw that in my face, and you think that I am so dumb that I don't pick up on when you are doing it. News flash Cherokee, I am not dumb. I am not normal, at least not yet. I had a plan, and it could have worked. You ruined everything; your body is compromised. I'll never be normal now, and its all your fault. I hate you. "You never make any sense, and I am so tired of trying to figure you out. I am tired of trying to fill in the blanks because you want to keep me in the dark. How is that protecting me? How is this even my fault? You are the one that got me pregnant. I didn't just get pregnant all by myself. How dare you talk to me in such a way. After everything that I've put up with, after everything that you've put me through. I have tried to do nothing but give you all of the love that I have. It is not easy to love you Ara, it really isn't. Despite the difficulty, I make an effort. I try to love you even when I don't want to. If I were anyone else, I would resent you, but I don't." There it is you keep doing it. You keep acting like you don't resent me, but you do. If you really didn't, you wouldn't keep bringing it up. You may try not to resent me, but that doesn't mean that you don't. You may try to love me, but all you are doing is just trying. You shouldn't have to try; it should just be. It's really quite simple. If you really loved me, you'd just love me. There shouldn't be so much trying and effort, it should be automatically occurring. That isn't the case though, and you just made that blatantly clear to me. But since you are finally being honest, I'll be honest too. I was trying to protect you but lets just stop all of the trying. You can either handle it, or you can't. Either way, like Alice said I am so tired of hiding parts of myself. I want to just be me, without second guessing if I'm being judged. I want to be me, even if it's scary.

And Cherokee, I am scary. You know that I know that apart of you is scared of me. Maybe a part of you really does love me, but it's not enough. There's too much complexity, and it's not what I want. I want you to love me without trying. I want you to accept me for me, without being afraid of me. You may not be bothered by my scary nature, but you are afraid of me. You are afraid that I will kill you. That feeling may not be on the surface, but you'd be lying if you said that it wasn't there. I won't even give you the opportunity to lie to me, because I don't know what I'll do if you lie to me right now. I don't feel like sparing you right now, I don't really even care about how you feel. Alice showed me something that I really needed to see, and I wish that I could have kept her around just a little longer. You made me kill her, and I resent *you* for that. I'm a killer Cherokee, it's just who I am. I like how it feels when I kill. I like being responsible for someone's last breath. I like feeling the terror that emits from their body the minute that they come to terms with the reality that they are dying. I like that, in fact I love that. I don't want to feel ashamed for that, because that's just who I am.

Why can't I embrace it? I'm not going to live a lie anymore. I am so tired of living a lie. Cherokee, I do love you, but I hate you too. Apart of me really cares for you and values your life. Another part of me is looking forward to the day that I can kill you. I'll miss you, I really will. But killing feels better than being with you. Killing feels better than anything. I'm tired of controlling my impulses for the sake of being a good or a normal boyfriend. I am not a normal boyfriend, and I think that you sensed that from the very beginning. You wanted something chaotic, that's what you were seeking. Whether you realize it or not, that's just what it is. You are broken, damaged goods. I liked that about you, I could see the shattered whimpers of your soul through your eyes. Maybe that Is one of the things that makes me so attracted to you. You have a hunger for chaos. You like being with someone like me, someone that's bad. You like that part of me, even though it scares you a little bit. You are only afraid because of your own life; you aren't afraid of what I'll do to other people. You are like me Cherokee; I see the potential killer in you. I studied humans for a really long time, since before your great grandparents were even thought of. I've spent my entire life completely fascinated with the humankind. I have dedicated my entire existence to the study of humans. That is why I am here. I am the most famous Moid in existence, yet I left the fame to come to earth. I know you better than you will ever know yourself. Don't try to tell me that I'm wrong. I was so close to achieving my ultimate goal. You were the perfect vessel, but you ruined it. Now I don't know what to do with you. "I wont disagree with you. I don't know if your right, because maybe you are. I don't know, and I don't really care. I'm pregnant, that's all that I can think about. But it sounds like you want to just throw me away. Whatever your sick twisted plans were got interrupted, and you are going to put all of the blame on me. You want to toss me to the curb because of what? I'm your perfect vessel? What does that even mean? What did you plan on doing with my body Ara?" Cherokee submits. Isn't it obvious? There has been nothing more that I've wanted in my entire life other than to be human. I have found a way to make my dream happen, and you could have helped me with that. But now you are pregnant and I can't do anything with a pregnant body. Not only are you pregnant, but you are having my baby. I am not human, therefor I don't know what your pregnancy will be like. Moids live extremely long lives, but our pregnancies are one of the most challenging aspects of our existence. Moid pregnancies last for only two weeks. The first week the mothers feel no symptoms nor are they showing. The second week the entire pregnancy speeds up and they experience five-minute contractions. The average human experiences around 90 seconds. I don't know how your body will react to the pregnancy. I do know that it will be very unpleasant for you. Your pregnancy could be extremely long, or it could be extremely short. There is no way to know this. I don't know how to fix your body once you have the baby. I don't know how I would be able to get it exactly how it was before. But I don't want a pregnant body, I want your current body. I was going to merge my soul with yours and reside in your body, basically like ghost or demonic possession. I found a way to make it happen, and I could be human. I could really be human. I wouldn't have to host in temporary bodies, your body is perfect. "Ara, please tell me that you are joking. Because there is no way that you really did all of this so you can possess my body. There is no way that you saw me in the mall that day, and thought to yourself that I would be the perfect body to snatch. There is just no way. Our whole relationship was built for the sole purpose of you hosting in my body. This is sick, this is worse than anything than I would have ever imagined. I would rather you just kill me." When I saw you, I was on the search for someone's body to make my own. That's where my head was. I never planned to really fall in love with you. I didn't even know that I was capable of loving in that way. I thought that you were the most beautiful girl in the world, and I wanted to be that. I wanted to be with you, but I also wanted to be you. I wanted to feel perfect. You surprised me with your love, I've never been loved in the way that you love me before. We created something special, a special bond. I knew that I didn't want to just take a hold of your body and hide away your soul. I wanted to become one with you. I wanted to your soul to blend into mine. I wanted to still feel you with me, which is why I bonded us together. We could have been so powerful. Your darkness and my darkness merged together would have made us unstoppable. You'd live on inside of me, and it wouldn't be much different then how things are now. You'd live inside my head; you'd have your own room. You'd have the space to be whatever you wanted to be without having to ever deal with the real world. Leave it up to me, I'll take on the world for you. At least that's how I thought it would go. That's what I wanted for us. What is more romantic then merging with your lover? Romeo and Juliette committed suicide right? I thought that we could take it up a notch, wed create history. Our bond is real, I don't appreciate that you are questioning it. Don't doubt us, we are invincible. We may hit bumps in the road but, we still have a special connection. Regardless of how we think we feel about one another, the connection is there. "You just continue to prove to me time and time again how delusional you are. You live in La La land Ara. You need to wake up and live in the real world with the rest of us. You are living a delusion; you are not well. I wanted to go along with whatever you had to say but I can't do it. I can't pretend that everything is fine when it isn't. You are a human being. I don't know what could create such a far-out delusion that you are some kind of other worldly being. You are just human; you've got to come to terms with that. You may not

like yourself, but I love you. I will help you learn to love yourself, but you have to drop the delusion. You have to wake up,
this isn't right. You have taken this way too far with the killing
and cannibalism. You are not some kind of vampire. You made
me drink your blood. You have to know that that isn't normal behavior." So, all of the sudden you don't believe me? You
don't believe anything that I've told you? You think I'm just
some psycho drinking peoples blood for kicks? Cherokee I really am disappointed in you. How do you explain the healing?
I healed you, with my blood. How else can you explain that?
How else can you explain coming back to life? No one else can
die and just come back to life. It's because we are bonded, I
have healed you. Human blood cannot do this. I can't believe
you right now, I thought I knew you but maybe I was wrong.
Maybe I have gotten you all wrong. You are pregnant with a
Moid! A Moid Cherokee, not a human baby. I don't think that
I should even have to prove to you that I am who I claim to
be. I thought that we had something special. What happened
to us? "Is that a joke? What happened to us? You've been drug-
ging me since the moment that I arrived here. You didn't think
that I knew that? You think I'm some kind of airhead? I'm not
Ara, I knew exactly what was going on. I knew that anything
that I thought that I saw was probably just a hallucination. You
know what isn't a hallucination though? My baby, my baby is
real. You raped me Ara and you got me pregnant. That was real, that is probably the realest thing that's happened." I'm sorry that you feel this way. I'm sorry that I did this to you. I'm
sorry that I've isolated you from society and caused you to lose
a few of your marbles. That's all on me. No human would be
able to live in these conditions without completely going nuts.

THE PERFECT VESSEL

I'm sorry Cherokee you have, you have completely gone nuts. I'm sorry that I'm going to do what I'm about to do. I'm sorry that this has all happened in the way that it has happened. I'm going to make it right, at least for me. I'm going to still find my perfect vessel. I'm going to leave you here to care for your baby while I restart my quest. I need to find the perfect vessel, and that is no longer you. You no longer have any value, its over Cherokee. "What are you breaking up with me? Because I don't believe your delusions? Because I was raped and got impregnated? That's rich, really Ara. You can't break up with me. We aren't even a real couple. We haven't been a real couple since the day that you forced me to be your prisoner. That's all I am Ara, I'm your prisoner." You don't mean that. Maybe it's just the fetus affecting your brain. "Do you hear yourself? You sound pathetic. It's a baby, can you say that? A baby, a baby that you put inside of me against my will." Don't do this, don't do this Cherokee. "Do what Ara? What am I doing? You a mess, and you know it." You were just crying because you were jealous that I paid too much attention to another girl. What was that all a show? "Ara, I just needed it to stop. It wasn't even really about her." You are lying to me Cherokee. I don't know what's going on, but you are lying to me. You want to see what happens when you lie to me? Is that what's going on? You want to see just how bad things can get? You want to walk on the edge of the cliff? You want to see if you'll live or die? Cherokee just stop it. The only one who is sick here, is you. Don't try to flip the script on me. It's not flattering on you, the lack of accountability. You look silly because you are such a bad liar. You could never be an actress, the only thing that you'd be good for is standing around in the background looking pretty. Don't push me Cherokee, because I will show you who I am. Although I'm tired of holding back my true nature for you, I do it anyway for your sake. You don't want to have the baby? Is that it? You want me to hurt you to try to terminate the fetus? You just found out that you are pregnant, and you already want to abandon your creation? Our creation, living proof of our love. "A baby is not living proof of love. Its proof of two people being irresponsible. A baby Is proof of two people not being prepared. It is proof that you raped me, because you did rape me, Ara." I hate you Cherokee, lets quit with all of the games. I just told you that I am tired of all of the trying. I am trying with every fiber of my being to hold my composure. Because you are trying to trigger me, you are trying to test me. I don't have it in me to keep playing games with you. Not now, not after I've lost my perfect vessel. "It doesn't feel good to be blamed now does it. Falsely accused of things that aren't rational. I'm tired of the arguing, if we were normal, we would spend more time loving each other. We barely even enjoy each other's company. We aren't a couple; in fact, we are nothing. Parents, that is all we are. Soon to be mommy and daddy. I hate that you did this to me. I hate you. I hate that I will never experience having a normal boyfriend because of you. I hate that I have to raise a baby in a place that I'm not even allowed to leave. It's all your fault, and I will never forgive you for it."

Cherokee didn't mean what she was saying, and Ara knew this. He knew that she was acting out on purpose, but it still drove him over the edge. He hit his breaking point and lost control. Cherokee knew exactly how to trigger him, because like he said they had a connection. They had a connection that bonded them together before the blood shed even began.

Cherokee wondered how many lives he took, but she never could muster up the courage to ask him. She wasn't afraid of the number; she was afraid of how he'd react to the question. During Cherokees stay with Ara he did unspeakable things to her. He inflicted her with excruciating pain as a way to keep himself out of the killing mood. Ara didn't want to kill people when he was with Cherokee, he really did want to be a good normal boyfriend. He'd slip up on occasion and come home and make love to her. She never knew what got him in such a passionate mood, but she liked when he would come home and toss her around like a ragdoll. She was his ragdoll, to do with whatever he pleased. He was a good lover and Cherokee loved that about him. She didn't care what got him so worked up that he would come home and create fireworks with her. She overlooked a lot of things for the sake of giving him the love that she felt that he needed. She felt that he was worthy of a good love, and Ara loved that about her. He never felt worthy of a love so pure, yet he was able to obtain it. When Cherokee pushed Ara passed his limits, she did it for her baby's sake. She didn't want her baby to be exposed to that life. Cherokee always wanted kids, but this wasn't the kind of life she wanted her kid to have. A life exposed to murder, torture and necrophilia. A life with no friends and never seeing the outside world. Cherokee was okay with this life for herself; she actually loved it, just not for her baby.

She sacrificed herself to try to save her baby. All she had to do was trigger his homicidal impulses, and she could be set free. She could join her baby in the afterlife and spend eternity with a healthy love. A love without fear and violence. A pure love that had never been exposed to the cruelties of life.

Ara grabs Cherokee by her ankles and drags her mannequin like body across the dirty floor. Cherokee didn't try to fight because she made this decision, she accepted her fate. Whatever it may be, Cherokee was prepared to make the sacrifice for her baby. Ara drags her to a dark room that she's never seen before. He tosses her body towards the back of the room. An infuriated. Ara flips the light switch on to expose a room filled with bulky chains hanging from the ceiling. Corpses hanging from some, but most of them just empty hanging. He showed Cherokee a room that he never anticipated on allowing her to see. Ara didn't know if he could really kill her without his blood in her system healing her and bringing her back to life. He was hungry for violence and was determined to create some kind of bloodshed. He knew that if she survived than they would never be the same again. He knew that their relationship was really over. He wished that they could have had a final conversation before he lost her. Not a fake argument, but a conversation with true shared feelings. He wanted her to break character for a moment and tell him she loved him, or goodbye at the very least. Instead, Cherokee stayed silent, she didn't murmur a word or move a muscle. Seeing her so committed to her role saddened Ara, but it also fueled his homicidal rage. He didn't scream or throw things around, he was calm. The anger brewed inside of him until it overflowed, but he remained calm in his demeaner. Ara grabs Cherokees dull body and takes the hook at the end of the chain and sticks it through her chest. Her body dangling from the air three feet off the ground. Cherokee completely submitted to the pain and doesn't make a sound. Her face scrunched up in agony refusing to let a peep fly out of her mouth. Ara grabs a stool and sits down to watch his lover bleed out. "It didn't have to be this way." He says in disappointment. Cherokee remained alive for 2 minutes but lost so much blood causing her to slip away. A tear falls down Ara's face as he watches her completely fade away. He remained in his seat pondering his life choices. Wondering what he could have done differently. His heart filled with doubt that Cherokee was the one. He thought that he made a mistake. If she was really the one, then things would've played out differently. After going back and forth with himself for a few minutes, he notices Cherokees pointer finger twitching. Her fingers start to slowly wiggle around. Her bloodshot red eyes intensely open with shock. Gasping for air, she turns her head in each direction getting an idea of her bearings. "You...you're alive. You're okay!" For now, Cherokee whispers. "I didn't know if you'd come back again" Well here I am. "I'm sorry for everything, I really am. I was so afraid that I wouldn't get to tell you I love you one last time. But I let the anger inside of me get the best of me. I'm going to work on it. I will be better for you. Let's have this baby, let's be parents. I don't want to toss you aside or experience life without you. I don't want your body; I'll find my own from somewhere else. You are my world; I don't want things to be like this. Can you forgive me for everything? Will you please have this baby with me? I don't want you to ever leave my side again. "I have an idea, which could solve this. Actually, it wasn't my idea I won't take the credit for it. Can you take me down from here I don't want to bleed out again." Sorry, right let's get you down and all cleaned up. "Thank you, I'll tell you about the idea. Help me wash up?" Cherokee says. "I'd love to, this is our fresh start. I know that it was a bit drastic, but we aren't like normal couples. We don't fight the same way that everyone else does, and I'm okay with that. I know that you are my home and I have to take care of my home. I promise things will be different. We may not be normal, but it will be our normal. Our new normal, especially with a baby joining our family.

Loosing you made me realize so much. Everything is going to be okay; I just know it. I'm going to make sure that you and the baby live the lives that you deserve. I'll even let you guys leave the house. Cherokee raises an eyebrow at a remorseful Ara. "Wow, you sound like a whole new person. Did I come back to some kind of parallel reality or something?" Very funny, I just learned a lot from your absence that's all.

Ara removes the hook out of Cherokees chest and gently places her feet on the ground. She struggled to stand on her own so Ara carries her into the bathroom. Cherokee feels worried that something was going on with the fetus because her womb felt different. She didn't want to say anything to Ara that would potentially ruin his out of character chipper mood, so she kept it to herself. When he placed her inside of the bathtub, blood started to drib down her legs. Her wound from the hook healed by the time they got into the bathroom, so she knew there was something wrong with the baby. "You are bleeding, didn't your wound heal?" It did, I don't know what's going on. I might have an idea as to what it could be, but I have to tell you something first. "You can tell me anything, but I'm worried." It's okay. When I died, I met someone. Someone really special. "Who was it?" It was our baby Ara. Our baby spoke to me. I saw her and she wanted me to tell you something. Don't worry it's not anything bad. Its good, at least she thinks so. I told her I was hesitant, but she insisted. She said that she knew the perfect vessel. She told me that it wasn't me, it was never meant to be me. I was only a bridge to be able to bring you the perfect vessel. "You saw our baby? She knows who my perfect vessel is? Well, who is it then? You are losing more blood, are you sure you're, okay?" I'll be fine, don't worry about me. Our baby Ara. Our baby girl said that she is your perfect vessel. She volunteered herself for you to merge with her. She was pretty insistent, she said that she wouldn't take no for an answer. She's different Ara, she's not human. She's special, the first of her kind. She is going to take your soul even if you don't agree. She is going to give you a powerful body. A body with immense power that no one has ever seen walk this earth before. You will be undetected, no one will ever suspect you. Think of what that'll mean. You'll never have to worry about getting caught, because you do know that killing is illegal. It's the perfect solution, our baby is your perfect vessel. She knows that you wanted to be human, but she is certain that the power that comes with this body will be better than being a boring human. She also wanted me to tell you that she loves you and she'll always be with you. "Our...our baby girl said that?" Ara's eyes fill with tears. He thinks it could be a good idea, but he's saddened that he'll never get to meet his daughter. "If she is insisting and won't take no for an answer then I guess I don't have much of a choice. So, did she mention how will this work? Will I still be me, even as a baby? Are you going to like...raise me? A supernatural phenomenon like this is new territory for me." She said not to worry about how it will happen and all of the ins and outs. You will learn when its time. She said that the minute that she comes out of me you guys will merge. There isn't anything that you have to do, she will take care of everything. "I guess you guys really talked this through huh? You weren't gone for that long, she really told you all of this?" Time is different over there, she just wants you to put your trust in her. "I trust her, that's my baby girl. I don't know her, but I trust her with my life. "Ara I think its time." She's coming? Like right now? I don't even see a bump, are you sure? "I'm sure, there wont be a bump. Powers remember? This is not a regular baby, and this is not a regular birth. She says that it won't hurt, she isn't going to hurt me. I love you Ara. I love our baby, and I'm sorry. I'm sorry for all of the times that we fought. I'm sorry for all of the troubles that we had. But we made it, and I'm happy that we did. I'm happy that we are going to bring a baby girl into this world, regardless of the odd circumstances." I love you too.

The baby slips out from in between Cherokees legs. A fetus the size of a mouse is revealed through the pool of blood. Cherokee looks at her baby, closes her eyes and slips away. Ara falls to the ground as his soul leaves his body and enters the baby. The old body rapidly ages and turns to ashes leaving the baby the last living person in the room. All of the blood that Cherokee consumed from Ara spilled out of her body during delivery, returning back all of her life-threatening wounds. Once Ara successfully merged with the baby, it starts to grow to the size of a normal baby. Left alone trapped in a baby's body unable to speak, Ara drinks all of the blood spilled in the bathtub from the delivery. His body begins to grow the more blood that he drinks. Once the blood is all gone; Ara ages to a four-year-old, now able to walk. He grabs the keys and locks up his former home, with a deceased Cherokee still inside with no burial. He walks through his property until he reaches a road for someone to be able to see him. A red Volkswagen pulls over to the side of the road to see why a child was on the side of the road. The kind woman gets out and frantically asks him why he's on the side of the road. "Mommy and daddy left me here." Ara says with an innocent voice.

The woman drives him to the closest police station to turn him in.

She leaves her contact information just in case if her help was needed. The police question Ara on his whereabouts, but he wouldn't speak to anyone. After bringing in social services and counselors to try to get Ara to speak about where he came from, they decided to call the woman that found him. When the lady returns, she asks him why he won't speak to anyone. He responds, "Mommy is dead and I want you to be my new mommy."

www.ingramcontent.com/pod-product-compliance
Lightning Source LLC
Chambersburg PA
CBHW031347160726
47993CB00002B/859